The Long Weekend

MIMI FLOOD

Copyright © 2018 Mimi Flood

All rights reserved.

This is a work of fiction. Names, characters, businesses, places, events, locales, and incidents are either the products of the author's imagination or used in a fictitious manner. Any resemblance to actual persons, living or dead, or actual events is purely coincidental.

ISBN: 978-1-7753539-0-4

Cover design: Isabelle Gariépy

Cover photo: https://www.pexels.com/photo/green-apple-6028/

For Mom, JP, and all those who kept pushing me,
you know who you are.

Wednesday, April 19th

CHAPTER ONE

It was a particularly rainy and chilly April evening. The last couple of days had been blessed with sun and a warm, southerly breeze. It was beginning to feel like spring, at least the kind of spring we have here in Montreal.

Tonight, however, the weather had taken a turn for the worst, as if foreboding bad times to come. Being prone to believe in signs, I had a feeling Mother Nature was, in fact, trying to warn me and that maybe I should have stayed home. Instead, I found myself walking into this ridiculously upscale restaurant.

"Reservation for Martinez," I said to the maître d' who greeted me.

He smiled and led me toward the back of the dark and under-lit establishment to our regular table. Paul loved this restaurant—their specialty was seafood, after all. He didn't mind much that I hated most seafood, so long as he got what he liked. Then again, I hadn't exactly objected when he suggested dinner here. I liked their lamb dish that came with mashed potatoes, tomatoes and peas. It didn't hurt that it was the most expensive thing on the menu so it would make a small dent in Paul's otherwise overfilled and overused wallet.

I sat down on the wooden chair which contrasted against

the modern, black and gold decor, and ordered some wine. The waiter soon appeared with a glass of nicely chilled Pinot Noir and a basket of bread. I started to nibble on bread, slowly filling my stomach, knowing that I wouldn't be hungry by the time Paul got here.

Later, I checked the time and saw that he was running late—a little over a half an hour. The waiter brought me a second glass of wine, this time avoiding eye contact. I was certain he was mocking me, probably thinking I had been stood up. I could imagine him walking back to the kitchen, wagering with his fellow waiters about how long it would take before I left, brokenhearted and defeated. Whether or not I would leave crying or with my head held high. Part of me wanted to join in on the bet.

Might as well make some money off my own misery.

I was becoming very aware of my surroundings—fellow couples, all whispers, and kisses, playing footsies under the table. The entire restaurant was the size of my apartment, which wasn't very big. I desperately wanted to leave, my gut telling me this wouldn't be one of our regular date nights. It was now eight o'clock—I'd been here since seven-thirty. I decided I would give him another fifteen minutes. Not one second more. Generous, really.

Then, as I felt him brush past me, my phone rang. The sound and its timing made me jump. It was my mother. I'd deal with her later, I told myself, sending her call to voice mail. Right now, I had to deal with him. He pulled out his chair with a loud scraping sound that made me cringe. I could never quite understand why someone obsessed with these haughty restaurants, and who was always concerned with his appearance, could be so unmannered and crass. It annoyed me, really, his disregard for social decorum. The air around me seemed to fill with tension along with subtle hints of his cologne.

"Damn work," he said, his version of an apology. "Have you been here long?"

"Since seven-thirty. You did say seven thirty," I reminded

him, annoyed. I noticed that he hadn't even bothered to give me a kiss.

"Right." Saying nothing more he sat down and picked up his menu, perusing it. I watched him, his deep blue eyes giving no hint of feeling sorry for having kept me waiting.

After a few moments, the waiter appeared, offering Paul the wine list. He was in mid-sentence before Paul interrupted and sent him away rather rudely.

"Listen, Lizzie," he began, taking a deep breath once the waiter was out of earshot.

I hated being called *Lizzie* and couldn't quite remember why or when I had let him start doing so. I could tell from his tone that Mother Nature had been right after all—shit was about to hit.

"I'm sorry to have to do this, but I don't think we're working out." The words came out so nonchalantly, so without emotion, that it took me a moment to be sure I'd heard right. "I'm sure you knew this was coming," he added.

He was right—I had known, or at least I had some inkling for a while. But having a feeling about something and having it manifest in front of you in public is another thing entirely.

Typical.

"Only you would bring me to a fancy restaurant, make me wait and all just to dump me," I snapped.

Why couldn't this have been done at my apartment or even at his for that matter? I chugged the rest of my wine, listening to his empty words about us hopefully being friends. I took a moment to look at him—really look at him. I saw past his looks, which were one of the things that kept me crawling back every time, and I focused on the real person behind those incredibly deceptive eyes. I accepted the fact that this time I was so thoroughly done with him and let the realization sink in.

By the time the waiter returned—only after casting nervous glances in our direction—I knew I had to leave. Without a word, I stood up, grabbing my coat and left the table. I could hear him unemphatically calling my name, probably not too happy with my reaction, and could tell people were curious despite their failed attempts at acting indifferent. I didn't mind if they watched—let them.

I got to the doors and stopped. Putting my coat on, getting ready to walk into the driving rain, I was surprised and stupidly disappointed that he wasn't coming after me. The eternal romantic inside me was somehow expecting him to come and stop me. My efforts were futile, I knew it, but the optimist within me kept hoping. I imagined he would rush over, grab me, apologize profusely for being a jerk and take me into a passionate embrace, making the fellow onlookers incredibly jealous. I knew that even if he did make such a gallant effort it would be insincere and wouldn't last, but I was a victim of cheesy romantic movies. I always looked for grandiose expressions of love—even when love had long since left the building.

I asked myself then if he did make some effort right now, would it change anything? I glanced back to our table. He was giving his order to the waiter, a small grin on his face. His lack of interest in me and our pathetic excuse for a relationship was all the answer I needed.

Asshole.

I stormed out into the cold, damp night, holding my coat tightly against me.

In a way, I was happy that the restaurant was a dozen or so blocks from my apartment. Sure, walking in five-inch heels through the stinging rain wasn't the most ideal of scenarios for a post-breakup walk, but the opportunity to go the long distance gave me the time to digest what had just happened.

I couldn't really blame him. I should have known better. After all, this wasn't our first breakup. By my last count, this would make it our third. I was the idiot who kept coming back. I was the one who, for some inexplicable reason, even when I could see the breakup was inevitable, stuck around just long enough to get dumped over and over. I was the one who always thought that maybe the next time things would be different.

Paul and I were finally over, I reminded myself, taking a deep breath. It had been a long time in the making, and let's face it, it was something I should have done a long time ago. I should have been the one to initiate the break-up but had been too chicken-shit to make the first move.

And now, here I was, stuck walking through puddles, feeling sorry for myself, wondering when I had given him all the power in our relationship. Why had I just left the restaurant without saying more, I wondered, shaking my head.

The bell rang above my head as I walked into the corner store. The owner, Mr. Nguyen, sat behind the counter, reading his newspaper as he did most evenings. He looked up at me and smiled, clearly noticing my soaked appearance but saying nothing about it. I headed toward the back wall, found the fridge that held the wine and, finding my regular, cheap but favourite bottle of white, I took it, ignoring my reflection.

On my way to the front, I grabbed a few chocolate bars and a bag of chips. I was starving, I now realized, having missed out on dinner.

Mr. Nguyen put down his paper and rang up my items. "Eighteen dollars."

I handed him a twenty.

"No umbrella?" he asked, handing me my change.

"Why would I need an umbrella," I answered snarky, putting my wallet in my purse.

"Silly lady," he said, laughing.

Part of me wanted to tell him to *fuck off*, but knowing his sense of humour too well, I simply smiled and thanked him. Braving the rainstorm, I returned out into the cold and rounded the corner to my apartment. The sooner I got into something dry and warm, the better.

CHAPTER TWO

Barely through my apartment door, I threw my purse on the floor and removed my now drenched coat, hanging it up. I walked to my tiny bathroom, ripped off my wet clothes and hung them on the shower curtain rod. Taking a towel from under the sink, I dried my hair a little and wrapped myself in my bathrobe.

I had only just turned off the light when I heard my phone ringing. Rummaging through my purse, I cursed at the amount of stuff I had in it, and, finally finding my phone, I read the caller ID. I had expected it to be Paul, saying he had yet again changed his mind and wanted to make up. I was surprised and relieved it wasn't.

"Hi, Dad," I answered. "First Mom, now you. Must be important." My tone was light but I was a little annoyed.

"Hi, Elizabeth, we need to talk," he said.

"Right. Is there any way it can wait until tomorrow? I've had a really shitty night and—"

"It's Grandma," he interrupted his words barely more than a whisper.

"What's wrong. Is she alright?" I was immediately hit with a bad feeling, my gut somehow instinctively knowing what he was about to say.

"No, Ellie. She passed away this morning."

My knees buckled and my legs gave out. Luckily, I was standing near a chair.

"How?" was all I could manage to say.

Sure, my grandmother was old, having just turned ninety-one, but she had been the image of good health only a few months prior. My brain quickly did the math and I realized a few months may have been closer to a year.

"The doctor says it's most likely natural causes."

Natural causes. I never understood how death could be caused naturally. At that moment nothing felt natural about it. I looked at the fridge and saw the yellow Post-It note with *Call Grandma!!!* scribbled in black marker. My heart sank a little deeper.

"She called me last week, told me she wanted to talk. I kept stalling to call her back." My voice cracked a little.

"I know, sweetie," my father said, consolingly. "The funeral is this weekend. Your mom and I were hoping you could maybe come down a little early to help with everything."

Still in shock at the news and trying desperately to clutch on to what remaining composure I had left.

I answered softly, "I'll drive down tomorrow."

"Good," I could hear the desperation in his voice, the sadness of losing his mother. My heart broke for him. "Thank you."

Though I wasn't sure, I felt that he might be crying. My father, always the epitome of strength and composure sounded so small and fragile. It shook me to my core.

"I'll be there, Dad." I hung up and threw the phone on the table.

The reality of the situation came crashing down on me within seconds, as did my emotions. Overwhelmed, I headed to the kitchen and dazedly poured myself a large glass of wine. Taking a deep breath, then a long gulp, I tried to calm down.

Ever since I had moved away from home, I had tried to focus on my life in the city. I had come to Montreal for school and, by now, had expected to be halfway around the world, living life fully, using my expensive education to make my dreams come true.

Instead, I was living in an over-priced and cramped apartment, with no real claim to anything. I worked as a freelance writer, which left me with far too much free time and far too little income. My only relationship that had lasted more than a few months had been with Paul and as tonight reinforced, had never been a very healthy one. And then there was my cat, Max, who crawled onto my lap, purring, rolling onto his side, expecting to be stroked. I smiled at him, through my tears, appreciating his unconditional love.

I was now alone, filled with such pain. Ironically, the one person I knew would be the best to talk to about this situation was now gone. The idea that I would never be able to speak to my grandmother again was incomprehensible.

Again, I saw the note on the fridge and shut my eyes, trying to remember the last time I'd heard her voice.

A week prior, she had called but I had been at Paul's place and wasn't interested in speaking with her at that exact moment, so she'd left a message. She had sounded sad, serious—which wasn't normally like her—and she had only said she needed to talk. It had been a long while since we had spoken or seen each other, so I assumed it was just an attempt to touch base. Whatever it was, her voice had given me the impression I should probably call back, hence the note on the fridge. In reality, I didn't need the note. I knew I should call her. But I didn't.

And now it was too late.

I walked to the fridge and ripped the note off, crumpling it and throwing it in the garbage. As if by coincidence, the doorbell rang.

Reluctantly, I placed the chain on the door and looked to see who it was. I wasn't that surprised when I saw Paul standing there, but still hesitated before unlocking the door. I was sure seeing him right now was by far the worst idea but at the same time, I was in desperate need of the company.

"Babe," he said through the closed door. "I'm sorry."

I had been through this so many times that I could already hear his regurgitated speech resonating in the back of my head.

"Please, let me in," he begged. Though subtle, I could hear the drunken slur in his words. He wasn't being too loud, but I knew the neighbours would soon open their doors out of curiosity. With a heavy sigh, I wiped the tears from my cheeks and despite my better judgement, I let him in.

His suit was wet, his hair dishevelled. I should have sent him on his way.

Sorry, not this time, buddy.

As he walked past me, I could smell the vodka mixed in with the rain, the cold, and his usual scent. Something within me shook and the familiar feeling confirmed my doubts. I shouldn't have let him in, especially not in the condition I was in.

"What do you want, Paul?" I asked, knowing full well what he would say.

He reached for my hand. "I don't want us to be over."

"You don't, do you?" I asked, sardonically.

Yanking my hand away, I walked toward the kitchen table and finished my drink in one swig.

"Want some?" I offered, getting myself a refill. knowing his visit might last a while.

"Sure," he said, removing his damp jacket.

I watched him peel it off slowly, revealing his soaked white shirt, which clung to his chiselled chest. *Look away*, I told myself, pouring him a measly glass of wine. The quicker he drank it, the quicker he would leave—at least that was my hope.

"I don't know what I want anymore," he said, taking the proffered glass. "But every time I think we're better off apart, I keep thinking that maybe we're not."

I stared at him in disbelief. Surely, these constant emotional twists and turns he went through were signs of something seriously wrong.

"Damn it, Paul!" I snapped. "I'm not going through this with you again." I was nearing the limits of my patience, which

I had to admit should have been reached ages ago. "Tonight is really not the night for this," I added, handing him a towel. I sat down on the couch, sinking into its softness.

He knelt down in front of me, drying his hair. "What's wrong?"

He seemed genuinely concerned, which was so unlike him. It was more than likely a ploy to get back in my good graces—a tactic that had sadly worked so many, many times before—but I fell for it anyhow. I felt rather vulnerable and appreciated having the shoulder to cry on, despite who it belonged to.

I told him about my grandmother, Dolores Williams. He looked at me as if he didn't understand my attachment—and why would he? Paul and I had been together for years, and he had never met my family or known much about them. He couldn't entirely be blamed for this, though. Paul's absence from my family's life was partly my doing.

Since I had moved from home I rarely visited them, and when I did, I preferred not to drag Paul along. He was as urban as it got and compared to my rural, bucolic family, he would just stick out too much. Then again, maybe I had kept him away from them because part of me knew we didn't really fit together and I knew that my family, especially my wise, perceptive grandmother, would see right through the charade that was our relationship. Whatever the reason, I had maybe mentioned Dolores to Paul at most two or three times. And each time was in passing, an anecdote. So understandably, he couldn't fully grasp how sad I was learning of her death.

Then again, had he ever bothered to ask about them, maybe he would be more aware. Paul, being who he was, usually focused on himself more than anyone else, had never shown much interest in my life before he came into it, especially not my family. He knew the general information: country girl moved to the city, found a job, lives alone. That was all that mattered to him, I suppose.

I was starting to question what I had ever seen in Paul. Other than his looks, which, I had to admit, were divine, his personality was starting to bug me and in all likelihood, probably always had.

"I never knew you were so close to her," he said, confirming my theory.

"Used to be close," I corrected, the admission killing me.

After graduating college, Dolores would call me weekly to see what I was up to. Nothing was going my way, friends were hard to find and I ended up working in a dentist's office, a job that, at the time, had grown much more permanent than I had originally intended it to. I was living a life that wasn't even remotely close to what I had envisioned, and especially not what I had bragged to my family was the reason I had to leave town—why I had to move to Montreal.

The fact that I had been so sure of myself before coming to the city, the way I had been so arrogant in my beliefs, turned me against my grandmother, and, not wanting to hear the disappointment in her voice every time she called, I slowly began to pull away. Soon, her phone calls diminished and eventually, our only conversations were when I spent the holidays at home. No doubt she was disappointed in me, as was the rest of my family, so I told myself over and over again that it was just easier avoiding them altogether.

Now, as reality hit, I quickly felt ashamed and regretful. I would never have the opportunity to speak to her again. What I wouldn't give to sit across from her and chat over a cup of tea. I would tell her about Paul, about the complicated relationship we had spent the last three years maintaining and ask her opinion. I knew it wouldn't be favourable, but still, I imagined she would have placated me and told me how to make it work.

Tears started rolling down my cheeks. I had never before shown this much emotion, if any, in front of Paul. I felt myself blushing, embarrassed.

"I'm sorry, Lizzie," he said, reaching up and using his thumb to wipe away my tears. For once, he was showing genuine sympathy and it caught me off guard.

Before I could stop, I took his face in my hands, finding his lips with my own. I knew it was probably the worst thing I could do at that moment, but I really didn't care enough to stop. I didn't want to face what I was feeling. I knew I was making a mistake, but all I craved was reassurance and to fill the void I now felt in the pit of my stomach.

Paul wasn't good for many things, and I was sure I would regret it in the morning, but all the same, at that precise moment, I needed the distraction. I needed *him*.

Thursday, April 20th

CHAPTER THREE

Paul had left at some point during the night.
Big surprise.
I couldn't be sure when he had gone, but I knew the sun hadn't fully risen yet. Through semi-closed eyes, I had watched him find his clothes and tiptoe cowardly out of my room. Part of me never wanted to see him again and wouldn't feel all that sad if I never did. I couldn't really be mad at him—it was to be expected. We had both gotten what we wanted out of each other and his sympathy from the previous night would never have lasted, that much I knew. Of course, I should have known better than thinking angry sex would solve our problems or relieve the heartache I felt.

Over a cup of coffee, I tried to erase the lingering memories of the tumultuous dreams I'd had; one of which left me with an especially haunted feeling—a feeling the caffeine wasn't shaking.

I had found myself floating in the middle of a large, open expanse of water. I had no recollection of how I had gotten there, just that I was in serious trouble. I felt panic in my chest, my breathing was laboured even though I wasn't moving. I was just floating, not on an object or raft, but on the open waters. When I eventually decided to swim for land, my limbs would not move no matter how much I told them to.

Suddenly, I felt like I had been lifted and placed on something that was keeping me above water—a piece of driftwood I assumed. I was still in the middle of nowhere, but I wasn't as scared this time. Peering over the edge of the raft, into the deep, dark water, I saw my reflection but not much else. Then, out of the murky depths, a white, almost translucent face appeared. Strangely, it didn't frighten me—quite the opposite. I gazed into the blue eyes set in the round face I recognized better than my own and immediately knew my grandmother was at peace and that everything would be alright.

Now, sitting at my small, round kitchen table, I felt drained and anxious, to say the least, the dream's feeling of peace having vanished.

My coffee cup drained, I didn't have much of an appetite, so I began attacking the to-do list I needed to complete before I could leave for my parents. I watered my plants, did my dishes, leaving the apartment nearly spotless.

I spoke quickly with Mrs. Benson, my neighbour, and asked her to take care of Max while I was gone. As usual, she accepted.

"My condolences, Elizabeth," she said, taking my hand. It was such a small thing, wrinkled and warm. It reminded me of my grandmother's and nearly made me jerk my hand away.

"Thank you," I replied, forcing the image of my dead grandmother from my mind. "I should be home in a few days."

She nodded and took the keys to my apartment.

"Not to worry. Take as long as it takes."

The drive out of the city was the distraction my brain craved. The highway, its straight and uncomplicated route which was engraved in my subconscious, meant I didn't need to focus on the directions as much as I would have wanted to. Instead, knowing precisely where I was going, my brain kept running back to the previous night, to my troubles with Paul, and most importantly, to the upcoming trial that was this weekend. Intent to not allow those thoughts to bog me down, I tried desperately to focus on the road ahead.

Once I was out of the city, leaving the malls and suburbs behind, the road became calm and the scenery more enjoyable. The road twisted and turned this way and that way, lined with tined-roof homes and old tractors set aside as if they had been forgotten. I drove past these farmhouses that were older than time itself, their wood siding faded and worn from years of wear, barely looking like they should still be standing, and yet, I smiled when I noticed the satellite dishes hung to the edges of their roofs. Though there were still some elements that brought back a simpler time, it was clear that even the farmers had been trying to leave that time behind.

I passed vast farmlands where cornfields were soon to be born and cows were grazing, the bumpy roads not used to cars but rather tractors, making my car thump with every bounce. The fresh air soon became overwhelmed by the smell of recently spread manure in the fields, forcing me to shut my windows.

In the distance, the silhouettes of the Appalachian mountain range, its peaks dwarfing the tall silos that seemed so huge, called me home like some kind of finish line. Somehow, the sights made the trip fly by. Soon, I was driving into my hometown—the small, idyllic town of Frelighsburg, with its population still hovering at just under three-thousand. I drove past the scant homes, separated by acres of farm fields, memories surging back into my mind. The towering trees that arched over the roads and formed lush tunnels, like some sort of welcoming committee, all indicated that I was only a few minutes from my parents' home. Sadly, being back for something as sad as my grandmother's funeral made what was once so vivid and beautiful seem dark and depressing.

I pulled into the driveway and parked the car. Immediately, my parents, Corinne and Alex Williams emerged from their home, my mother looking grief-stricken despite the heavy coating of make-up, my father's sorrow painfully obvious. They looked older since the last time we had seen each other, I thought, which wasn't that long ago. They seemed so different. My father had bags under his eyes, the darkened skin giving his blue eyes an eerie look and the small lines on my mother's face, which used to give her face some character, were now menacingly taking over.

My father took me in his arms, rather by surprise.

"Hi, Honey."

"Hi, Dad," I replied, stunned at his show of affection. He had never been what I would call a very lovey-dovey person, but considering the circumstances we were now in, I let him hold me. I stayed there, encompassed by his strong arms, a little unsure what to do or say next.

"Take it easy on her, Alex," my mom said, her tone severe. At least she seemed her normal self, I thought. My father stepped away allowing her to hug me. It felt cold and distant, as it almost always did.

"Hi, Mom."

"Come, let's go inside."

CHAPTER FOUR

My father held the door for me and I was hit with the familiar smells of my childhood home—a mix of vanilla and pears. The scent brought back feelings and memories I wasn't in the mood to face, so I shook them away as quickly as they entered.

"I love the wallpaper," I said, pointing out the newly renovated foyer.

"It was your mom's choice. I thought it was fine the way it was."

"Oh, Alex, you'd be happy if this entire house still looked like it was built in the sixties." Though she was trying to sound playful, the edge to my mom's tone made it hard for me to laugh along. "Elizabeth, your room is ready for you, if you want to go and get settled."

Taking the hint, I went upstairs to what had once been my bedroom. Years before, it had been the perfect example of a room where a teenage girl growing up in the nineties' would call home. I had pasted the walls with heartthrobs and rock bands, leaving barely any signs of the pale, pink colour I had begged my father to paint when I was eight.

They had changed everything shortly after I had moved out when I was eighteen. They had never told me of their plans, leaving me to be surprised the following Christmas on my return home for the holidays. My feelings had been hurt, to say the least, but I had never brought it up. There would have been no point.

Now, all signs of my old bedroom were long gone, replaced by a guest room that contained a small, glass desk in one corner and an elliptical machine tucked in the other.

Dropping my bag on the floor with a heavy thud, I sat on the bed and looked around. At least the walls were still that pale pink, bringing back memories from years ago of a happier time before all the other crap had happened and things got so complicated.

I couldn't let those memories haunt me, especially not now. I was here for my grandmother and I had to stay focused. Now was not the time to dig up the past. The guest room—my bedroom—was starting to feel smaller than it really was. With a sigh, I decided to join my parents downstairs.

My mother was in the kitchen making lunch—extremely complicated and gourmet sandwiches, from the look of it. She pointed her chin toward the back veranda where my father was sitting, his shoulders hunched, the epitome of a broken man.

"Go talk to him," she suggested.

Again, I got the impression she was blowing me off, getting me to go elsewhere which was a common feeling I had when I came home, but I wasn't about to point it out. I didn't want to fight with her and I knew I should take some time with my dad, anyhow, so I joined him outside.

The door squeaked as I walked out onto the screened-in porch. The veranda overlooked a large lake which was about thirty feet below. Growing up, this had been my preferred part of the house. From it, I could see straight across the lake to my grandmother's house, at the top of the opposite hill. Her house now seemed lifeless, almost as if its essence had disappeared along with her. The orchards that surrounded her home, with their over two-hundred acres of land, were just starting to come to life, the apple trees revealing their springtime blooms. The leaves were out, still glistening with the morning's dew.

Small white and pink blossoms were beginning to emerge. Seeing my grandmother's favourite time of year in full swing and realizing she had just missed it broke my heart. Life's timing sucked sometimes.

"Beautiful, isn't it," my father whispered. It was more of a statement than a question.

"Sure," I replied, nodding.

As a teenager, I had never truly appreciated the beauty and quietness of my surroundings. Then again, what teenager would? My father had tried to make me see it, to make me appreciate it, but I would always belittle it. It wasn't rare for me to make fun of its insignificant existence or even claim its population was made up of inbred farmers—present company excluded, of course. My desire to live in the city, to be as far away as possible from small-town folks had started early. Now, maybe because of my years spent in the city and my jaded perspective on things, or maybe because of being let down by the lacklustre life I was living, I found the scenery put me at ease and I was overcome by a longing for the peace it provided.

I wasn't about to admit it to my dad, though.

"What are you going to do with it all?"

Being her only son, I assumed that Dolores had left her home and the orchards to my father. I also assumed he was probably completely overwhelmed by the sudden and new obligation.

He let out a small grunt but didn't stop staring out across the water. He had never been a man of many words, so I didn't think much of it. It was more than likely a response to the entire shock of it all. His mother was gone and to top it all off, he was now faced with the responsibility of caring for her entire life's work, the *Williams' Family Orchard*.

Originally started in the forties, the orchard was the brainchild of Dolores and her husband, my late grandfather, Albert. My grandmother had inherited the land from her father shortly after she had gotten married and my grandparents began planting the trees that now made up the orchard.

Through years of dedication and hard work, Dolores and Albert had created one of the largest and most successful apple orchards in the province.

Now, the company was flourishing and ever-expanding, selling their products across the world. Despite the constant pressure to buy out competitors and use their lands and warehouses, my grandmother insisted they keep to their original roots as much as possible. So, even today, over seventy years after its beginnings, the company ran everything from right across the lake.

Of course, my grandmother had inevitably conceded and built larger warehouses but she still remained in her home and ran things like she had when she had been a young girl of seventeen. Even when my grandfather had passed, which had been a terribly hard time for her, she had found a way to overcome her grief and work through it. Her resolve to keep the company thriving was inspiring to watch and in a way, had motivated me. Though I had shown no interest in the orchards or joining the family business, her work ethic was definitely something I wanted to emulate.

Reality brought me back to the present and I knew that with both founding members gone, the orchard's legacy was now left in the hands of my father, a high school science teacher who had never shown much interest in the business either. I couldn't quite see him being fit for the task at hand and knew that his silence and the slight look of panic on his face was probably from his own realization of the magnitude set upon him.

My father spoke as if sensing my eyes on him.

"Not sure how this will all play out."

"What do you mean?"

"You know. Everything."

I still had no idea what he meant. Was he thinking about all the responsibilities he now faced? Surely he had spoken to his mother about the inevitable day when she would pass and this would be his to take care of. This couldn't have been a complete shock to him. Then again, there was something about his distant look and his choice of words that made me think there was more to all this.

"What's going on, Dad?"

He looked over at me, finally making eye contact. He seemed tired and unwilling to delve into what was bothering him. He took a deep breath as if he was about to speak when my mom shouted from inside, telling us lunch was ready.

"Shall we?" my father said, getting up from his chair, looking relieved for the interruption.

He walked into the house and I knew the chance to hear whatever he was about to say had vanished.

CHAPTER FIVE

My mother didn't hesitate to put me to work in the afternoon and my time was spent helping her organize the remaining funeral details. Luckily for all of us concerned, nothing—not one detail—was left to chance thanks to Dolores' minutely organized preparations. She had left detailed lists which contained all her wishes and every element had been clearly described and taken care of beforehand. A long time prior, my parents had received a letter wherein Dolores had broken down what was to be known as her Death Party into a point-form checklist.

Now, as I skimmed through the list, seeing what needed to be done, and what my mother had already managed to accomplish by herself, I was only left with the minuscule task of calling a few of my grandmother's friends. Still, something as simple as telling them when and where the party would be was turning into slow torture for me. Their grief, their fears at being next in line, their simple near-deafness, all made me feel more anxious and unsteady than I already had that day.

Still, I pushed through, and as I hung up on the last guest, I let out a deep, cleansing breath. The air inside the house was stifling nonetheless. Despite my failed attempts at small talk, my mother seemed to be keeping her emotions and thoughts to herself.

"Dad seems to be taking it reasonably well, all things considered," I said once in between phone calls.

"It seems that way," she agreed, seeming unsure.

"How about you, how are you doing?"

"I'm alright, don't worry about me," she snapped, picking up the phone and dialing.

I knew that was as much as she would say, at least to me. It was stupid of me to expect my normally tight-lipped mother to suddenly open up and share how she was feeling. Still, I kept trying, continually expecting a different outcome only to be disappointed.

I decided to go for a walk, desperately needing some fresh air, to stretch my legs and to get away from the tension in the room. I headed down the steps toward the lake, crouching to dip my fingers into the still slightly frigid water. Seeing my father's kayak parked on the beach, I decided to take it for a little ride. I paddled a few feet from the beach and let the gentle breeze do most of the work. It wouldn't have taken long to paddle the lake's entire circumference, but I wasn't looking for exercise, just some alone time with my thoughts. Passing our neighbours homes, I wondered how many of them I would see over the weekend. I worried about the questions they would ask, the gossip that might start.

My thoughts were interrupted when I found myself passing in front of a particular house. The people who lived there would definitely be at the wake, I thought, my gut clenching with nerves. The house, which stuck out from all the rest, had been slowly transformed over the years, but since I last visited my parents, the home had gone through some serious renovations. It was now so stunning, it could have easily graced the cover of *Architectural Digest*.

Its entire lakefront had been landscaped into a true thing of beauty. A large, brick fire pit was surrounded by stone walls as if it was hidden in its own private nook. Zigzagging steps made their way up the grassy slope to the house, which was now utterly breathtaking. The lake-facing wall consisted solely of windows and the owners had added a second storey to the bungalow. Inside, was a large living room with an immense stone fireplace as its central focal point, and a modern, all-white kitchen.

The Barretts, the family who lived there, had never seemed like the kind of people who would like that style of home. I began to wonder if maybe they had retired early and moved out, allowing the new owners to make these changes. Then again, maybe I was wrong. I hadn't known them that well. It still didn't make sense to me that David and Micheline Barrett would have turned their once boring but traditional bungalow into such an open and contemporary home.

David Barrett, the father, was tall, handsome and had always been friendly with my parents, though never a close friend. His wife Micheline, was petite and blond and kept to her gardening. Though they had been quiet neighbours and kept mostly to themselves, they were always kind on the rare occasions where we had interacted. I remembered their daughter Valerie and how she had always seemed awkward and shy, and with three years between us, we had never become friends.

And then there was Devon, their son. A small shiver went through me as his name popped in my head. Though I hadn't seen him in a long time, every detail of him came back crystal clear in my mind.

He was tall, had brown hair that was streaked with subtle hints of blond and had the most captivating green eyes. His skin was a delicious caramel colour, and even in the dead of winter, he somehow retained his summer complexion.

Summers had been my favourite time of year because they gave me the opportunity to watch him swimming in the lake or playing football with his friends, oblivious of my affection. He was only a year older than me, but we had lived in absolute opposite universes. He was unbelievably gorgeous, popular and a jock. I had spent most days watching him from a distance, secretly pining for him, but had always been too shy to approach him. I kept to my quiet shell, focusing on my writing and other interests, all the while daydreaming that he and I could one day be more.

My kayak slowed down as it approached the shore of the Barrett home, snapping me out of my daydream. I started to paddle away when a flicker of something in the top window caught my eye. The sun had started to set and the glare forced me to squint in order to see properly. I didn't know why I was looking—I probably seemed like a peeping tom—but something kept me from looking away. Once my eyes adjusted, as if deciphering a hidden object in a 3D painting, I gasped.

A man, with a toned and chiselled body, was standing at the window completely naked for the whole world to see. A part of me knew I should row away, but instead, I found myself frozen, watching, using my oar to keep me steady. I couldn't deny that his body was hard not to look at. A feeling of familiarity came over me and my mind immediately flashed to Devon and his body.

Could that be him?

He seemed the right age, his skin did have that same, sun-kissed colour. The last I had heard, Devon had moved away a few years after I had and hadn't been back since.

No sooner did the thought pop into my head did the man look directly in my direction. I panicked, uncertain what to do. Surely he couldn't see me, I reasoned. Why else would he be standing there if he knew someone was watching him? I was too far down to know for sure. His expression didn't change so I assumed he was actually looking elsewhere and hadn't spotted me. Relieved, I slowly began to manoeuvre the kayak around, back toward home.

Feeling slightly embarrassed, as well as a little flustered, I walked up the hill, shaking my head in disbelief. I kept seeing the man's features and wondering if it could have been Devon all grown up. The sun had prevented me from getting a good look at his face but his body, well, it was definitely a grown man's body. The last time I had seen Devon shirtless he had been a teenager—albeit an incredibly muscular one. But then it occurred to me that Devon would now be thirty-one. If that was him in the window, did that mean he had returned to Frelighsburg? Was he now living with his parents?

A million questions were running through my mind. My father was sitting on the veranda yet again, drinking a beer. Pulling up a chair beside him, he handed me a can from the small icebox he kept at his side. I thanked him and took a long, hearty swig. The fizz burned my nose and eyes, but I didn't care. I needed to settle my nerves a little after what had just happened.

"Nice ride?"

"Nice, yes," I replied shyly. We sat in silence, watching the still water, the soft breeze in the trees. This time, I was happy that my father wasn't known for his conversation skills.

"Dinner will be ready in thirty," he informed me, breaking the silence. I stood to go get washed up, maybe take a cold shower to erase the image of the man next door, when my father added, "We're having guests."

"Great," I said, less than remotely excited to have to socialize.

CHAPTER SIX

From my room, where I had been hiding, skimming through old yearbooks that, as chance would have it, my parents had been kind enough to have kept, I heard the doorbell and reluctantly headed downstairs.

My mom was already at the door, greeting the couple that stood there. Roger and Marie Longpré, long-time friends of my parents, were offering their condolences. I attempted to sneak by, but Roger spotted me before I could.

"Elizabeth?" he asked, unable to hide his shock.

I forced a smile as Marie took me into her arms.

"Look how much you've changed!" she said, her tone making it seem as if the last time she had seen me I had been in training bras and not just a few years. Uncomfortable with the attention, I cleared my throat.

"Come, let's not just stand here all night," my mother said, leading everyone into the kitchen.

I followed behind, already wishing this evening was over. Marie handed a bottle of red wine to my father who looked at it appraisingly.

"Excellent choice, as always, Marie," he said, smiling. Though Marie didn't seem to take notice, I could tell he wasn't being honest. Something about his demeanour seemed strange.

I couldn't be sure, but it felt like something other than his mother's passing was bothering him.

"You know me," Marie bragged. "Ever the wine connoisseur."

While they began to wax poetic about different wines and vintages, I took advantage of the distraction, and, taking the utensils and napkins from the kitchen counter, made my way to the dining room to set the table.

I had just finished rearranging things for the umpteenth time when I heard the doorbell ring yet again. I could hear my mother opening the door, kisses being exchanged, but I couldn't recognize the voices. I stood by the table, uncomfortably reorganizing things that were perfectly fine, my way of dealing with my nerves, I assume, preparing myself for whomever else was about to come in.

"And I'm sure you remember our daughter, Elizabeth?" I heard my mother say.

She walked in with our newly arrived guests. Immediately, the blood rushed to my cheeks and my knees went weak. There, standing a few feet from me in my parents' dining room was none other than the naked man I had seen earlier. Fortunately, now he was fully dressed in dark jeans paired with a light blue shirt with the sleeves rolled up to his elbows. His skin was tanned. In fact, it had retained that same familiar caramel colour. And his hair was golden-copper.

Just as I had remembered.

My stomach tensed and my knees shook as I struggled to come to grips with the thoughts competing within my head. I tried desperately not to imagine him naked, but it was proving to be impossible. Through my discomfort, though, I noticed the way he was looking at me with his piercing green eyes. They seemed to twinkle with their own recognition.

"Hi," he said, revealing the most beautiful smile, his voice deep and sensual.

My brain took its time to accept the fact that the man I had seen naked was, in fact, my high school crush, Devon Barrett. My mouth wouldn't cooperate. I stood motionless, completely aware of his extended hand but finding myself unable to move.

"Elizabeth, where are your manners?" my mother snapped. "Forgive my daughter, she's usually a hermit and isn't used to speaking with people."

I looked at her, trying to hide my embarrassment with a grin. It had never ceased to amaze me how sometimes she could be so kind, and yet at others, she could be so rude. I had never admitted it to her, but it had always bothered me to no end when I was growing up. Especially when that rudeness was aimed at me, such as now.

"Hi, I'm Valerie," said the tall blond girl standing next to Devon, obviously sensing the tension between my mother and me.

I shook her hand, finally finding control of my body. Valerie, Devon's younger sister, had aged, obviously, since the last time I had seen her. She was no longer the scrawny teenager with braces but was now a strikingly beautiful twenty-something-year-old woman. She had silky blond hair that ran bone straight down to her lower back. Her skin was similar to that of a porcelain doll, showing barely any signs of the horrible acne she used to have. Her teeth, a glowing example of the successful years of brace-wearing, were straight and perfectly white. She had truly grown into a stunning woman.

Standing next to her I soon felt very insecure about myself. My hair was up in a boring ponytail and I had barely put on any makeup. It wasn't like I had known who our dinner guests would be. Along with black jeans and a plain, white t-shirt, my whole appearance felt entirely inferior compared to her.

She held my hand reassuringly as if she could feel my discomfort. It felt like her amazing kindness was radiating through her and into me. I suddenly felt calm and happy.

"Do you remember my brother, Devon?" she asked, reintroducing him. He smiled and extended his arm once more. This time, feeling more at ease—and especially not wanting to look like a complete moron—I accepted it. His grip was firm but his hand felt soft and warm, sending a small shiver through me.

"I can't help but think we've met before," he said, giving me a small wink.

My breath caught as I dropped his hand.

"Must be from school," I replied dismissively, turning away so that he wouldn't see the embarrassment on my face.

At that precise moment, I would have gladly welcomed a sinkhole beneath my feet. Instead, dinner was served.

"Great, everyone's here," my father interrupted, walking into the dining room carrying a platter. "Let's eat!"

In an attempt to sit as far away from Devon as possible, I waited until everyone sat down. Inevitably, I ended up with the seat across from him. Better than being right next to him, I thought. However, as I sat down I realized he was still too close for my comfort. I told myself to simply avoid eye contact and to only speak to him if absolutely necessary. Soon enough, dinner would be over and I could retreat back to my room and try to forget any of this had ever happened.

I ate in silence, only speaking when spoken to, which was not often. Luckily for me, my parents monopolized the conversation. Nonetheless, I could feel Devon constantly staring at me, making me feel incredibly uncomfortable. I accepted the fact that he had probably seen me looking through his window, but I also reminded myself that he was the one who had walked around naked for the whole world to see. Why wasn't he the embarrassed one? To the contrary, he seemed completely unbothered. And what was more unsettling was the fact that this situation was making me so nervous.

Still, as he continued to watch me, I became more and more aware that embarrassed was the last thing he was feeling. It felt as if he was challenging me to do something. To do what, I wasn't sure. Was he planning on bringing it up or did he want me to say something about it? Was he daring me to make things awkward for him and I both? Was he trying to figure out just how much I had seen, or worse, was he looking for a sign of my interest?

I couldn't deny that seeing him after so many years, especially in the nude, had ignited many mixed feelings. On the one hand, I was taken back to my teenage years, when I had been completely infatuated with him—to a time when I had felt a rush when he looked at me and in those brief moments I believed there might be some mutual attraction. Unfortunately, that rush would never last very long and would always be replaced with the feeling of heartbreak brought on by unrequited love.

Yet, on the other hand, seeing him walk around in the nude—getting just enough of a glimpse at his body—had turned me on in a way I hadn't felt in a long time. Though I had been unable to see every single part of his body, I had seen enough to wet my appetite. Sure, Paul's body was great, but where he was lean and fit, like a runner, Devon was strong and sturdy. The image of his chest and washboard stomach came running back to me. His thick thighs, standing assertively at the window, made me squeeze my legs together.

Coming back to my parents' dining room, I rubbed the bridge of my nose, hoping it would help dissolve the pictures of him. My thoughts kept shifting from those of a socially awkward teenager with zero experience to a sexually attuned and definitely aroused adult. As this tug-of-war raged in my head, I desperately hoped my face wasn't giving away my thoughts. I kept avoiding his eyes—a feat unlike any other I had faced in recent history—and maintained my composure until dinner was done.

"So, Elizabeth," Roger said, catching me by surprise. "What have you been up to?"

Everyone's eyes turned to me, waiting for my answer.

Shit.

"Working, keeping busy," I said in an attempt to answer without needing to go into further detail.

"Elizabeth is such a hard worker," my mother pitched in. "She works so hard, she barely has time for her own family."

"Corinne, really," my dad interjected, putting his hand on hers. "Elizabeth's job is time-consuming and I'm sure she's just been very busy. I wouldn't take it personally if I were you."

I bit my tongue, trying desperately to avoid the fight my

mom was clearly looking to start. My father smiled at me then, making me feel a little more reassured, but I still didn't feel great.

The fact was that he was wrong—I hadn't been that busy. I could have visited more or at the very least definitely called more. The truth was that my mom was mad at me for other reasons. Her outburst tonight was just one example of her passive way of attacking me instead of calling me out about something that was bothering her. I knew better than to let her goad me into a fight, and so I sipped my wine, hoping someone would come to my rescue.

"What is it that you do, Ellie?" Devon asked, my knight in shining armour. He smiled knowingly.

Hearing his voice, I nearly choked on my wine but maintained my composure.

"I'm a freelance writer."

"Anything I would have read?"

I heard my mother's stifled cough but chose to ignore her.

"Probably not. I work mainly on company websites and online newspapers."

"She's the next Charles Dickens," my mom joked, her tone malicious.

"Christ Mom, how much wine have you had?" I snapped, unable to stop myself.

"That sounds really interesting," Devon added, completely unphased by and ignoring my mother's interruption. "I've always envied writers. How they're able to put into words what others only feel in their hearts."

"Well said," Roger added, raising his glass. "To writers, freelance and all."

I raised my glass along with everyone, feeling good for the sudden burst of support even though it was nearly impossible to ignore my mother rolling her eyes.

I gave Devon a smile, thanking him without saying a word. He smiled back and nodded subtly in return.

CHAPTER SEVEN

My mom and I had managed to remain civil enough to make it through supper and dessert. While she and Marie cleared the table, Roger and my dad sipped their coffees and chatted about hockey. I fiddled with my napkin, my conversation with Devon and Valerie having shrivelled down to nothing.

"Want to go for a walk?" Valerie eventually suggested to Devon and me.

Though the thought of prolonging my time with Devon didn't seem like a good idea, the idea of a stroll appealed to me greatly, especially when the counteroffer involved talking sports with my dad or even getting stuck doing dishes with my mother.

We left the house and walked down toward the lake. I was struck by memories of nightly walks I had shared with my grandmother when I was younger.

We would walk, arm in arm, and I would share every little problem I was having. I now knew my minuscule problems were probably laughable at the time but she had always acted as if I was facing the most life-altering events. She would offer up the best advice and, from matters of the heart and petty fights with friends, she never once made me feel like what I was dealing with wasn't important. From an early age, my grandmother had been one of my best friends and until this very moment, I hadn't truly realized how much I was going to miss her and I could feel the depths of my grief opening up.

Tonight, however, instead of some deep, meaningful conversation, I was stuck with Valerie who was rambling about everything and anything—from the latest on *Twitter* to her hopes of finding Mister Right.

I nodded and pretended to be listening, but was more curious about Devon, who was slowly and quietly walking beside me, looking uninterested in our conversation. Slightly bored with whatever topic Valerie was discussing, I stopped in my steps.

"I was curious," I interrupted. "How come your parents didn't come tonight? I would have loved to talk to them about what they've done to the house. It's stunning."

Valerie froze, her eyes suddenly filled with sadness.

"You know? I'm a bit cold," Valerie said, wrapping her arms around herself. "If you don't mind, I think I'm going to head home." Without any other words, she turned and walked away.

"What did I say?" I looked at Devon, seeking some explanation.

He shook his head. "Don't worry about it," Devon explained. He started to walk again as he spoke—an open invitation for me to follow. " I guess you didn't know. Our parents died a few years ago. Car crash."

It was said so matter-of-factly, I wasn't entirely sure I had heard right.

"Devon, I am so sorry," I said, feeling the inadequacy of my words. "I had no idea." I reached for him, placing my hand on his arm in some kind of sympathetic gesture.

He nodded and told me how it had happened.

On a regular Friday night, his parents, who had gone out to celebrate their thirtieth wedding anniversary, had been struck by a drunk driver. I couldn't help but notice that while he told me about this horrible time in his life, he appeared to be at peace with his loss. "I moved back home after it happened, Valerie was a complete mess. She needed to move out, but I figured I would use the money they left to fix up the house—make it how they would have liked it to be had they had the chance."

"That's amazing, Devon. I'm not sure I would have done the same." I knew more than definitely that I wouldn't put any effort into my parents' home if I were ever in that kind of situation. "I'm sure they would be incredibly proud of the work you've done."

He smiled at me and shrugged. "That's the thing about death, especially when it comes out of nowhere. You really have no clue how you'll react. Not until you're in it."

"I suppose not. But then again, I'm pretty sure I'd just sell their house and move on."

"That's a bit harsh," he said, creasing his brow. "It's their home, their life. Would you be that thoughtless?"

"Thoughtless?" I replied, stunned that he suddenly seemed so judgemental. "Not everyone has a great relationship with their parents." My tone was a little more defensive than I had intended but his look and the way he had spoken to me had rubbed me the wrong way. "You're lucky that you loved your parents so much and that you wanted to honour their memory. I wish I could feel the same."

"Why do you hate your parents?"

"I don't hate them," I nearly shouted. I didn't like the direction our conversation was headed. "It's a long story."

"I've got time," he said. "After what I saw tonight, you don't seem to be in the best of places with your mom, that's for sure."

Where was he going with this?

I didn't want to get into the deficiencies of my relationship with my parents and especially not with him—a man I barely knew.

"Can we just drop this, please?" I walked ahead of him, annoyed.

"Absolutely." His expression made it seem as if he was

enjoying arguing with me. "But really, if you ever want to talk to someone, I'm here."

Before I had any time to react to his proposition, which felt like more than just a friendly offer to chat, we had reached the summit of the hill. Nestled between a large cluster of apple trees, we found ourselves in a small clearing of a few square feet wide. I looked around, puzzled. Throughout my countless walks through these orchards, not once had I ever been to this place.

"Why aren't there any trees here?" I asked, bewildered by the random bareness surrounding us.

"No idea. Trees have never grown here," Devon explained, pointing toward the lake. "But it's nature's best seat in the house, that's for sure."

I followed his eye line and understood what he meant. From our vantage point, we had an undisturbed view all the way to the lake.

"On nights like this, I come here and I can just sit for hours. There is something appealing about it. It's like I'm hidden from everything."

The night was incredibly clear and crisp, the moon's reflection bouncing off the still waters below. The best part about this spot, at least in my mind, was the privacy it allowed. Though we could see everything, the angle of it made it so that no one else could see us. Tucked into its little nook it was the perfect hiding place. I couldn't understand how I had never stumbled on it before. I certainly would have found it magical as a child.

Devon sat down, wrapping his arms around his knees, inviting me to sit with him, which I did. Unsure of what to say, I remained quiet and took in the view. With a deep breath, I was able to relax a little, the beauty of the location seeping into my core. I had virtually forgotten about our little spat if I could even call it that.

"Look," he said, breaking the silence, "I'm sorry about before."

I nodded, a little surprised by his apology.

"It's alright. It's just complicated for me and my parents. I'm not sure what I would do in that situation."

"I'm not sorry about that," he said, interrupting. I looked at him, unsure what he meant until it came rushing back to me. He was talking about seeing him naked. I cringed at how quickly I had forgotten. "I was talking about this afternoon, you on the lake."

"Oh, that," I said, thankful he couldn't see my face in the darkness. "So, you could see me?"

He gave me a small nod. I could see a grin forming at the corner of his mouth.

"Do you usually do that sort of thing? Walk around naked?" The picture of his body popped into my head, again.

He laughed. It was such a delightful, melodic sound. "Actually, I do."

I was stunned by his candour. "Why don't you get curtains?"

"Why would I want to deprive people of this?" He indicated his body, but it was clear he was joking around. He didn't seem serious or come off as vain, so it made me laugh. "Besides, I'm more concerned with people feeling the need to look than what is or isn't covering my window."

He turned to face me now, his eyebrows arched.

"It wasn't like that. You were there when I looked up and, well, I don't know." I stuttered, words failing me.

Did he really think I had intentionally looked through his window?

"Relax," he said, stroking my arm and laughing softly. "I'm only messing with you."

We both laughed then, my laughter sounding nervous. The feeling of release it gave me, along with the simplicity of sitting next to Devon, made me feel more relaxed than I had been all day. I didn't know what it was about him, but something about him filled me with a feeling of calm just like his sister had done. Maybe it was in their genes. Whatever it was, I felt as if the tension had broken between the two of us and leaning back, I gazed up at the sky. I could feel his eyes on me.

"Elle, can I ask you a question?" he whispered.

The sound of his voice and the way my name seemed to roll off his tongue gave me chills and a warm feeling deep in my stomach. Maybe it was due to the deep, sultriness of his voice but I found I really enjoyed the sound of my name when he said it. I realized then that, strangely, no one had ever called me *Elle* before. I had always been *Ellie* or *Elizabeth* or my least favourite, *Lizzie*, a particular favourite of Paul's. Now, I found that I really loved Devon's choice.

"Sure," I replied. "As long as it's not about you being an exhibitionist, then I'm all ears."

"An exhibitionist?" he laughed. "No, that's not what I was going to ask." I wasn't sure but it felt like he'd moved closer to me. "I wanted to know if you were this cute in high school?"

I looked at him to see if he was joking again. His face wasn't showing any signs of kidding around. I laughed it off.

"Very funny."

"I'm dead serious." Then, his hand found its way to my knee, his thumb gently caressing it. He had definitely moved closer. "I don't remember you being this sexy and I'm wondering how I could have missed it."

His touch was making me tingle all over. My throat went dry. I started to think of all the times I had wanted to approach him but had been too afraid to. I remembered all the times he had walked right past me in the school hallways, not even acknowledging my existence.

As much as I wanted to say these things to him now, instead all I could manage was, "Are you fucking with me?"

"No, I'm not *fucking* with you," he grinned devilishly as he repeated my words back to me. I met his gaze. Even in the moonlight, I could see the green of his eyes, calling out something deep within me. I felt the blood surging beneath my skin as his hand ran up my thigh.

I froze, uncertain what to do. *Should I let this continue?*

I had to admit the setting was more than perfect and the images of what I had seen earlier that day made it incredibly difficult to not want to see more up close. Yet, as he started to lean in for a kiss, my pesky inner voice told me it wasn't a good idea. No, not because of what might still be lingering between Paul and me, but rather because I didn't know Devon. Sure, he had been the leading man in many of my fantasies as a teenager, and yes, he did have the most heavenly body I had seen outside of a magazine, but still, I didn't know what kind of person he had become. And I wasn't the kind of person who would sleep with someone she barely knew, no matter how insanely gorgeous he was.

"Devon..." I said, looking down, tearing my eyes away from his. His face was so close to mine, but he stopped. "Sorry, I've got a lot on my mind and this—,"

"—Don't apologize. I understand," he interrupted, letting out a heavy sigh and pulled away.

His sudden distance from me made me aware of the chill in the night's air. I sat back up and rubbed my hands together for warmth.

"You know, there is a good way for us to keep warm," he said, nudging my shoulder with his. I knew he was kidding again. "Want me to walk you home?"

I was cold and wouldn't have minded being indoors, but I was also slightly disappointed that he wanted to cut our evening short. Then again, maybe I had been right to stop him from making a move. Maybe that was all he wanted from me, in which case it was all the more reason to keep things platonic.

"I guess," I answered, reluctantly taking his outreached hand.

The walk back wasn't a very long one, but with neither one of us speaking, it seemed like miles. Reaching the bottom steps that led to the house, we both paused awkwardly. Everything now felt like a first date.

What exactly had just happened?

I started to question my reluctance to kissing him.

"Goodnight, Elle," Devon said quietly, leaning in to kiss me on the cheek. The warmth of his lips on my cold skin made my knees weak. "Sweet dreams."

With his mouth lingering ever so close to my ear, all the

reservations I had just moments ago flew away with the breeze. I wanted to take back my stupid words and tell him I was more than willing to let him make my fantasies come true. I was even willing to take him to my bedroom and have my way with him right then and there. Had I not been staying under the same roof as my parents, I just might have.

Instead, finding some inhuman resolve buried deep within me, I wished him a good night and watched him walk away. I saw him disappear into the shadows and sighed, feeling melancholic. I couldn't understand why I now felt so downhearted. How had I gone from breaking up with Paul, sick of men in general, to not wanting to do anything but follow Devon home and do unspeakable things to him? Someone I barely even knew, I reminded myself. Chalking it up to the unrequited crush I had never quite gotten over in high school, I shook off how I felt and dragged myself into the house.

Stepping inside, it felt warm and the smell of tonight's dinner still lingered. I could hear my parents and their guests in the living room, sounding a little tipsy, which was great for me as it gave me the chance to sneak by unnoticed.

I went upstairs to my bedroom, put on my pyjamas and got into bed. It was early, not yet ten o'clock, but I felt surprisingly tired and drained. I quickly drifted off to sleep. Unfortunately, an uneasy slumber awaited me yet again.

However, instead of haunting nightmares, this time I found myself dreaming of Devon wearing very little clothing if any at all. And every single time, I woke up in a sweat, my heart racing and my body screaming for more.

Friday, April 21st

CHAPTER EIGHT

"Elizabeth, wake up!" my mother yelled, abruptly jerking me out of my sleep. I shifted in bed and realized that last night's events had led me to forget to set my alarm. Shaking off the rather erotic dream I had just had featuring a certain copper-haired neighbour, I got out of bed and walked to the bathroom to splash some cold water on my face.

Hurriedly, I got dressed and ready. At first, I decided to forego any makeup but as I was leaving the room, I caught my reflection in the mirror and thought otherwise. My hair was dishevelled but the waves gave me a messy yet cute look I could tolerate. Quickly, I applied some foundation and a touch of lipstick. It wasn't much but it was enough considering the small possibility of bumping into Devon again.

My mother was frantic; gathering things, cleaning up what must have been breakfast. Noticing that she had left nothing for me, I poured a cup of coffee from what was leftover in the pot. The percolator had recently been turned off, I noticed.

"Mom, do I really need to go with you today?" I asked, putting my cup in the microwave to reheat.

We were headed to the reading of my grandmother's will and I didn't see the point of hearing her dying wishes. I knew too well who would get what, and I assumed I would be closer to the end of the list, the happy recipient of some old knick-knacks or possibly some jewelry I would never wear. Above all that, though, I didn't feel like being reminded just yet of everything my grandmother had left behind.

My mother stopped in her steps, looking at me with such displeasure I immediately wished I could take the words back.

"You are coming with us. That's final."

"Sorry. Forget I said anything," I apologized, taking my coffee and a muffin out to the veranda.

Clearly, she was still in the same mood as the previous evening and I really didn't feel up to sparring with her.

"We leave in five minutes," she added, as I walked away.

It was quite warm out, the sun very bright, and hardly a cloud in the sky. Compared to the previous night, it felt like a completely different season. The coffee was far too weak for my liking, not nearly bold enough to get rid of the drowsiness still lingering, but I drank it just the same.

Rubbing my eyes, I found I was unable to stop myself from glancing to my right, to Devon's house. Through the trees, I could just see enough of his house. I was hoping for something, but for what, I wasn't sure. Maybe for a glimpse of him on his deck, standing in the sunlight, sipping his coffee, looking as confused as I was? Whatever it was—and I was sure it could be blamed on my dreams the previous night—I felt that I desperately wanted to see him again.

I started hoping that maybe I would accidentally bump into him later on that day, but then started to panic when I thought about what I would even say or do if I did? Making the first move had never been my forte. But before that, before even contemplating how I would approach him, I had to remind myself that there was no point. I had to pull myself back to the present and the issue at hand. I wasn't here for him or to start anything. I was here for my grandmother. And no matter how enticing the idea of being with Devon was, I had to leave what had happened the previous night behind me. I had to acknowledge the way I was feeling for what it was: a crush, pure and simple. And as most of my crushes had done in the past, this one would eventually fade as well.

My mother knocked on the window and gestured to her watch. It was time to get this done and over with. I finished my muffin, swallowing down the last, dry mouthful with coffee, and brushed the crumbs off my lap. I would be heading back home in a day or two, leaving all this behind. Going back to my routine, my job, my friends, and to whatever else my life was made up of. Why was I pining for someone I would more than likely never see again?

Don't get involved, I reminded myself.

Situated in a one-hundred-year-old house, the notary's office was decorated in a very cold and modern way, which contrasted the house's Victorian style.

We sat in the waiting area, welcomed by an overly made-up middle-aged receptionist. She offered us a beverage and I quickly requested an Espresso, as strong as she had. While I waited for my coffee, I noted how silent my parents remained. Other than a word or two in the car, they hadn't spoken much if at all that morning. Something was definitely off.

Mr. Henri Charbonneau, the notary, soon greeted us. He was a young man, possibly in his late thirties, dressed impeccably well, his dark hair showing slight hints of white. His smile was wide and bright, and though I found him to be quite attractive, I was immediately turned off by the intensity of his cologne. I couldn't but compare his overpowering scent to Devon's clean, subtle scent. For some reason, I could almost recall it perfectly. Closing my eyes, I chased the thought from my mind.

We followed Henri into his office. The receptionist brought us our drinks and we sat down on extremely firm, brown wingback leather chairs.

"Corinne, Alex, yet again, I am so sorry for your loss," Henri began, informally. He then looked at me as if he had just noticed I was there. "Elizabeth, my condolences." I smiled, curtly. "Dolores truly was a magnificent woman."

He seemed like an honest man, but something in the way he had said *magnificent* gave me the impression he was laying it on a bit thick. He went on endlessly about how long he had known my grandmother, as well as both my parents while fiddling with a very fancy looking pen. He seemed nervous, making me think that maybe this was his first time dealing with such a substantial estate.

Clearing his throat, Henri opened a large, leather-bound ledger. "Let's begin," he said.

After spending several minutes reading through numerous paragraphs of legal jargon, most of which went right over my head, he finally got to the distribution of my grandmother's assets. The majority of her belongings, clothing and other trinkets were given to her friends or employees. Her collection of jewelry was to be given to my mother, something that brought a bittersweet smile to her face. *She'll be pleased*, I thought, remembering my mother's interest in a certain pair of diamond studded earrings.

I was beginning to worry that my grandmother had forgotten about me or had simply decided to cut me out of her will entirely. The list of items was starting to run thin.

Henri paused and took a deep breath. He looked us all in the eye, hesitating as if gauging our mood.

"What is it?" my father asked, clearly as puzzled as I was.

Henri bit his lower lip, giving him a childish and unprofessional look. His silence and the way his eyes shifted from my mother to my father and back again, made it clear a war was waging in his mind. Whatever was written on that paper was making him incredibly uncertain about how to proceed.

Just say it, I wanted to scream.

"Forgive me, but you must understand that these were her wishes," he explained before continuing with the reading:

"I, Dolores Williams, of sound mind and judgement, bequeath the ownership of Williams Family Orchards, as well as all possessions

and responsibilities therein, including and not limited to the residence situated at 36 Ash Lane, to my granddaughter, Ms. Elizabeth Veronique Williams."

Though I could see his lips moving, I couldn't for the life of me understand what he was saying. *There was just no way.* I must have misunderstood.

"Wait a minute," I interrupted. My parents, who appeared as confused as I felt, looked at me. "Did you just say my grandmother left the orchards…to me?"

"Yes," Henri confirmed, clearing his throat again. "As well as her house."

He smiled rather forcefully and looked at my parents. They both sat perfectly still, like statues. Though my father's face gave nothing away, my mother seemed to be having trouble controlling the panic attack that was growing beneath her otherwise calm exterior.

"Dolores has left you this letter, Elizabeth." Henri handed me a crisp, white envelope, with *Ellie* written on its front in my grandmother's unmistakable cursive handwriting. "I am certain it explains everything and will answer any questions you might have."

My hand shook as I reached for the letter. I was more than certain the letter wouldn't answer every question I had but thanked him nonetheless, too stunned to say much else. Henri finished up the reading, covering mostly small, unimportant details that didn't affect me directly, or in truth, I couldn't really hear. My thoughts were elsewhere, panic and disbelief having taken over, making his words sound like gibberish.

We left the office in uncomfortable silence, I wished I had my taken my own car. What I wouldn't give for a moment alone to absorb the last hour's information. So many questions were running through my head.

I knew I would eventually have to read the letter, but the idea of it, of seeing my grandmother's final words to me, made me queasy. And to be honest, I was in shock.

How could she leave me the Orchards?

The fact that this was probably why she had wanted to talk to me a week earlier hit me like I was walking into a brick wall. I felt the ground beneath me drop. The backseat of my parents' sedan caught me.

"Well, that was interesting," my father said, shutting the passenger door. "Are you going to read it?"

"Alex, please," my mother snapped, "It's none of our business what's in that letter."

She was watching me in the rear-view mirror, her smile not quite reaching her eyes. She sounded patient and sympathetic, but I knew better. Something about the way she was looking at me gave me the impression she was just as eager to have more answers and I couldn't blame her. I knew very well she was dying to know why Dolores hadn't left the orchards to them, which to me was the rational thing to do.

I ran my fingers over the envelope and the indented writing, willing myself to understand what the hell my grandmother had been thinking.

I couldn't wait to get home so I could read the letter in private, though I had a feeling that would be easier said than done.

CHAPTER NINE

Once we were home, my parents left me alone, wandering off to their respective hideouts, with their heads hanging, barely speaking to one another. The day was beautiful. It was a perfect spring day and the sun was shining. I decided to go by the lake rather than locking myself indoors.

Lost in my thoughts, I sat in a chair and took a deep breath. I looked at the envelope in my hands. Since getting it, I had been so stressed and anxious that I had nearly crumpled the sides from holding it so tight. Delicately as possible, I opened the top flap as if tearing it too quickly would somehow destroy it and make it vanish. Inside was cream-coloured stationery I recognized as my grandmother's. Tears filled my eyes as I unfolded it slowly and read her last words to me:

My dearest Elizabeth,

If you are reading this then I am dead. I've always wanted to say that! Now that I've brought a smile to your face, let's get on with it.

Yes, my dear, I have left you my home, my farm; everything of real importance. I am absolutely certain that you are angry, upset and no doubt wondering if I was suffering from dementia when I decided this. The answer simply is no.

I did not come to this decision lightly. The orchards are my life, as you know, and I could not leave them in the hands of just anyone. The company needs someone who will appreciate its importance and its value. It needs someone who will understand the work needed. Your parents, though they are good people, should not be left in charge. I cannot go into detail as to why, but you know better than most, I am sure. They have worked their whole lives and now, more than ever, need to focus on each other.

You, I believe, are the perfect match for the company your grandfather and I worked so hard to create. I am sure at this very moment you are doubting your capabilities. Please don't.

Do not take this opportunity lightly and please consider all your options before coming to a decision. If in the end, you decide this isn't for you, then so be it. If you do sadly decide to forfeit this gift, Henri is ready to help you with all the hassle.

I am sorry we did not have a chance to speak about this in person. That was my failing. I do not blame you. In youth, we often need space. We need to find our own way, make our own mistakes. I should have made an effort to bring you home more often. I do not have any regrets except for not doing so.

Please give this offer your most serious and sincere consideration. This is <u>all</u> I am asking of you.

I love you, Grandma

My head was spinning. *All I am asking of you.* It was written as if she was asking the simplest of favours. As if she needed me to water her plants! There was simply no way I could take on this responsibility.

What could she have been thinking?

My hands began to shake, my heart rate quickened and breathing became more and more difficult. Was I having a panic attack? I quickly put my head between my knees and tried to take deep breaths, overwhelmed by a nauseous feeling.

"Are you alright?" a warm and familiar voice asked.

Though I felt my insides tense, he was quite possibly the last person I wanted to see at that moment and especially in the condition I was in.

"Not really, no," I answered, keeping my head down, hoping this horrible feeling would soon subside.

Without looking at up, I handed Devon the letter. He was quiet for a time and then sat down next to me, rubbing my back gently, trying to comfort me. His touch surprised me, but it felt amazing.

"I figured as much," he said, making my head jolt up. "Dolores and I had talked about it a while back. Wasn't sure if she had already told you or not. I guess she hadn't."

"No, she hadn't! What do you mean you talked about it?" I snapped, the words coming out harshly. His answer had caught me off guard and I found I was unable to hide my frustration. "No offence, but why exactly would she have talked to you about this?"

He looked at me, confused as if I should know the answer.

"Because I'm the manager."

"What? But I thought you just moved back, after your parents…" I stopped, not wanting to bring up such a sore subject again.

"I did," he began explaining. "Right after graduation, I worked for Dolores here and there—helping out around the farm, you know, shit work."

I knew exactly what *shit work* meant in the Orchard's world. It meant picking out the bad apples, it meant boxing and crating. It basically meant disgusting and hard work that most well-seasoned workers didn't want to do.

"Then, I moved away for a few years. When my parents died, I came back and Dolores offered me a job as manager. Since I didn't have much of a choice but to stick around, I figured why not?"

"Right, why not?" I added, sarcastically.

I knew how this town could suck people in and force them to stay. It was the main reason I decided to move away as soon as I could. I felt bad for Devon in a way, being forced to return to Frelighsburg and then having to stay. Then again, he had accepted the job. It had been his choice.

"I had to stay, Ellie," he said as if reading my thoughts. "Valerie couldn't deal with everything that needed to be done once Mom and Dad were gone. And it wasn't so bad, really. I didn't have much going on in my life anyway."

"You didn't have a career or a girlfriend?" I asked, trying not to sound obvious. I was pleased that we were having a regular conversation and I wanted to know more about him. I didn't feel awkward around him, as I'd been afraid would be the case.

He chuckled, "Definitely no girlfriend. At least nothing serious." He picked up a flat stone off the ground and threw it into the lake, making it skip across the water. "I was working construction. Odd jobs here and there. Nothing stable."

"I get why you worked for her, but that doesn't explain why she told you all of this," I said, waving the letter in my hand. "And if she told you, why couldn't she tell me?" I remembered her voice on the phone message she had left me and how important it had sounded. I'd brushed it off as unimportant. Again, I was swamped by guilt.

"I didn't just work for her," he began. "When I moved back, I tried to be strong, you know, for Val, but your grandmother saw through that. She could see I was hurting. She helped me through it." He smiled, his eyes looking up across the lake at my grandmother's house as if reminiscing on a happier time. "Honestly, I don't think I would be here now if it wasn't for her."

Memories of her generosity toward others came flooding back, my eyes stinging with tears. My heart broke a little then as I thought about how I had been selfish. I had never given any thought to how her death was affecting others. In my foolish mind, it was limited to me and my immediate family. Obviously, she had played an important role in Devon's life and most likely in others as well. Let's face it—he had been present in her life far more than I had been, especially of late.

Still, I was angered—by the letter, by his admission, by everything. I could accept that my grandmother had been a key player in his life, but I didn't like knowing she'd kept secrets from me and that she'd clearly been much more open with Devon.

"Couldn't you be doing something better though? Somewhere else?"

I felt that circumstances beyond his control had forced Devon to stay and I couldn't deny the similarity between him and me. I was now facing this responsibility that I wanted no part of but which would undoubtedly drag me back, too.

"Better? I like what I do. Either way, I owed it to her to stay. Toward the end, she kept saying she wouldn't be around much longer, despite everyone thinking she'd outlive us all."

He looked down, his face visibly overwhelmed by darkness. Filled with empathy and without any hesitation, I reached for his hand, somewhat surprised by my own boldness. He paused, watching my fingers wrap around his, but didn't pull away.

"One day, she mentioned you and started talking about how much she admired you. How she admired your strength and courage."

I laughed and rolled my eyes. "I sincerely doubt that."

He looked at me, furrowing his brow. "You really need to work on that, you know?"

"Work on what?"

"This assumption you make that people are lying to you."

"It's not an assumption. People lie."

"I'm not sure who made you believe that, but I'm not lying to you, Elle. Dolores thought the world of you."

"Maybe, you believe that, but the truth is I disappointed her," I stated. "I let her down."

"I don't think that could be farther from the truth." He smiled reassuringly, squeezing my hand. Until that moment, his hand in mine had felt so natural, I had forgotten I was holding it.

I gestured toward the hundreds of acres of land with my free hand. "To leave me all of that though? That's absurd."

"I learnt a long time ago never to question the decisions of the mighty Mrs. Dolores Williams," he laughed. "She must have known what she was doing. Why are you doubting her?"

I shrugged not knowing what to say. He had a point. My doubts weren't stemming from my lack of confidence in her. My hesitation was coming from somewhere else but I wasn't about to start dissecting it. If I did, I knew that box would never get closed again.

We sat quietly, Devon's words echoing in my brain, his fingers running along mine. The feeling felt right and instinctual, but despite the comfort it brought me, I also longed for some solitude. Though I felt comfortable with Devon next to me, I still felt I needed a chance to think over everything I had just learnt.

As if reading my mind, Devon stood up, releasing my hand.

"See you at the party?"

"Party?" I asked, still slightly in a confused daze.

"*Dolores Williams' Death Party. Come one, come all!*" Devon said, quoting the invitation's tag-line, which had been chosen by Dolores herself.

With the morning's unexpected news I had let it completely drop out of my mind. Now, on top of this new information I had to digest, I also needed to be on my best behaviour and see plenty of faces that I thought were buried in my past.

"Wouldn't miss it," I said, with a reluctant smile.

"Great," he said, sounding pleased. "I'll see you there."

With a wink, he left and I watched him walk away. It was a pleasant sight, as pleasant as my dark mood would allow.

I need a drink, I thought and headed home.

CHAPTER TEN

A loud bang woke me from my afternoon nap. I was disoriented. It took me a moment to realize that I had fallen asleep on my parent's living room sofa. Sitting up, I massaged my temples, trying to ease my headache.

After I had spoken with Devon, I had come in to find the house empty. I had poured myself a glass of wine, which had turned into a few and feeling the strain of the day, I had shut my eyes for a moment. Apparently, that moment had turned into a few hours. I looked at my watch—it was now past six o'clock. I rushed upstairs, brushed out my tangled hair and applied some lipstick. I decided to change out of my wrinkled shirt and into a soft, light blue blouse I thought paired well with my black pants.

Heading out, I walked along the lake and up to Dolores' house. The sun had just started to set, the lake was now basking in the twilight, and the sky was various shades of pink, orange and blue. The house, which I then realized was now technically mine, was buzzing with the sound of people inside. The lights from indoors gave it a ghostly glow. I took a deep breath and walked up toward the back porch.

A group of people, most of them smoking, was gathered outside. Making my way through them and their clouds of smoke, I walked into the house via the opened French doors that lead into the den. There were a few faces I didn't recognize but the majority were immediately familiar. As if I had travelled in time, I saw many people I had known in high school but luckily for me, most of the guests seemed too enthralled with each others' conversations to realize I was even there or acknowledge my presence.

In the hallway, separating the den from the kitchen, I stopped in front of a large, framed picture. It made me laugh. It was a drawing I had made for my grandmother when I was seven. It featured my parents, my grandparents and myself, standing in the orchard, surrounded by extremely bright green trees filled with disproportionately sized red apples. The sun was yellow and had a smiley face. Everyone in the drawing had their stick arms stretched out, holding hands with their neighbour. I was at the centre, my grandparents on either side of me.

All too aware of the many people surrounding me, most of which were strangers, I swallowed the ball of emotion that rose up in my throat and continued toward the kitchen.

The room was the epitome of country style, with a large butcher-block island dead centre and copper pots hanging above it. The immense and fully functional old-fashioned range still stood against the white brick backsplash wall, as if it was proving just how mighty it was. Various plants were scattered throughout the kitchen, the perfect example of Dolores' green thumb.

A long table had been set up against the window that looked out onto the orchard. On it was a wide range of appetizers, all of which had been ordered a few days before and prepared by Marie and Roger, or rather by the staff at their restaurant. The food looked so decadent and delicious, I found that I was a little hungrier than earlier so I filled a small plate with mini quiche and some vegetables.

I took my food to the bay window seat, sitting down and observing the small crowd that walked in to replenish their empty plates. They were laughing and being much louder than one would expect people to be at a vigil. I felt like this was definitely more like a party than a solemn wake. In the middle of the group, I spotted a woman who was getting all the attention; Nicole Ratté. She had been the popular girl in high school. She was my age and much to my dismay, she had also been Devon's girlfriend on and off for years.

I watched her, loathing simmering under my calm exterior. Her wavy auburn hair glistened as it always had. Somehow it now seemed even more full and beautiful than it used to be. She was laughing that silly, girlish laugh, that had always made the boys hover and the girls roll their eyes.

Was it possible I still hated her?

Surely I had grown out of it and was too old to still be jealous of her.

"Ellie?" a blond-haired man asked, stepping in front of me, blocking my view of Nicole. It took me a second to place him—he had changed so much.

"Brian?" I asked, accepting his hug. I felt myself stiffen, ill at ease.

Brian Thomas had been my best friend at school. We had been nearly inseparable but once I had decided to move to Montreal, we slowly started to grow apart. So much so, that once I was in my second year of university, we had stopped speaking entirely. I had always felt that I was entirely to blame for not maintaining our friendship, and now, the seemingly forced hug he gave me seemed to confirm he felt the same.

He pulled away and I took him in. He had lost at least one hundred pounds since the last time I had seen him, but he looked fit and his platinum blond hair remained unchanged. He introduced me to the tall, dark-skinned man he was with, who happened to be his fiancé, Marc, and they both offered me their condolences.

"She really was a great woman, wasn't she?" Brian said while Marc nodded sympathetically beside him.

"She was," I agreed, trying desperately to ignore the sound of Nicole's laughter in the background. "So, when is the wedding?"

I had hoped the question would get him going and it did. Soon, Brian was divulging all the details and drowning Nicole out as much as possible.

"We were so excited about it but I don't know what we're supposed to do now," Brian said, overcome with apparent disappointment.

"What do you mean?" I asked. "Do about what?"

Brian looked hesitant and Marc tugged on his arm.

"Honey, this isn't the place to talk about it," Marc said.

"Talk about what?"

"See, the thing is, a few months ago, Dolores had offered to let us use her home for our wedding," Brian explained. Marc couldn't help but show his disapproval.

"And?" I asked, still not understanding why they were so uncomfortable.

They exchanged looks with one another and then returned to me.

"Well, now that she's gone, we'll have to find a different location."

"Which is completely fine," Marc added.

"Oh, yes, completely fine," Brian repeated. "It's just a shame she won't be around to see the wedding. I know she was excited about it."

Again, I found myself unawares.

Was my grandmother lending her home out for a wedding?

It was like I didn't know her at all. And here was yet another person who had been present in her life, had shared something with her, and I had known nothing about it.

"I'm still not getting where the problem is. Why can't you have the wedding here?"

Brian looked at me as if the answer was obvious. "It doesn't seem right to, now that she's not here."

"Don't be ridiculous. You are more than welcomed to have it here."

"But we couldn't impose, not now," he looked nervously at Marc as if begging for some backup. Marc kept his eyes on me.

"No, really, I insist," I said to the both of them. "She'd

want it this way. And this is apparently my place now, so it's really up to me."

"Your place?" Brian asked.

I explained about the inheritance. They seemed relieved they would still have a venue for their wedding, but Brian seemed to be hiding something.

"What is it?"

"I guess I'm just having trouble seeing you stick around and manage all this. I mean, it's kind of bizarre that Dolores would trust *you* with it."

Marc cleared his throat. "Brian, don't."

Brian looked at him and then became the image of sympathy and understanding. "No, don't get me wrong, I am sure you can do it. I just meant...never mind, it's not important."

I let out a nervous giggle, trying to ignore the blatant undertone of criticism Brian was throwing at me. I guess my assumptions had been right and he wasn't entirely over how I'd failed him and our friendship. He was still holding onto some hard feelings and to tell the truth, he was absolutely right to.

Brian continued, "Marc, did I ever tell you how obsessed Ellie was with that guy?"

I knew who he was talking about, but spun my head around anyway. Nicole partially blocked my view, but her hands were all over the man in question. Immediately, I spotted Devon's familiar frame. My heart began to race and that unpleasant feeling had returned. I watched Nicole put her greedy hands all over him. I had no idea what they were talking about but it seemed obvious that whatever Devon was saying was making Nicole laugh a little too hard. She was wrapping her arm around him, leaning her head on his shoulder and worst of all, he was letting her. His smile said so much.

It became obvious to me that there was something going on between the two of them and a huge part of me started to get angry that he hadn't mentioned it the night before when he had clearly tried to make a move on me. Even today, by the lake, he had never mentioned a girlfriend. *Nothing serious*, he had said.

Turns out I had been right—Devon was still a player. I felt so stupid. And after that morning, after the closeness we had shared, how could I have let my guard down so quickly and foolishly? And more importantly, why was I letting this bother me so much.

"God, he's so gorgeous," Brian said.

"Watch it," Marc warned playfully, taking his boyfriend's hand and squeezing it.

"Are they dating?" I asked.

"I see some things haven't changed," Brian teased, winking at me. I shook my head at the implication but he didn't seem to notice. "This week, who knows? Those two are like Ross and Rachel."

"Meaning?"

"Meaning they are perpetually stuck in a *will-they-won't-they* world."

"So then nothing has changed since high school?"

He shook his head and laughed. "No, not really."

I knew I shouldn't feel jealous, but at the same time, I could feel small parts of me lighting up with insane and illogical envy. Brian and Marc continued talking, leaving me on the outskirts of the conversation. I nodded along occasionally, but deep down, all I wanted was the chance to get Devon alone and find out the truth for myself.

CHAPTER ELEVEN

The noise from the party was getting to be a little too much for me to handle. I didn't feel at ease in such a crowded space, receiving condolences from people I didn't even know or care to remember. I began to feel trapped and so I went upstairs, at first just trying to get away from it all but eventually finding myself walking down the hall toward my grandmother's room.

The door was slightly ajar and I nearly knocked from habit before realizing there was no reason to. The room was dark, but the smell was the same—my grandmother's lilac perfume subtly lingering as if she had just been there, spraying some on her wrist as she always did. I hesitated before walking in, still feeling like I was doing something forbidden. Shutting the door behind me, I flipped the switch on the wall and the lamp in the corner turned on.

Everything was still, unmoved, and again I felt as if my grandmother had just stepped out for a moment. Her things were strewn across her vanity table, a brush left haphazardly next to some lipstick and cream. Her bed was made—not surprising since she never left the house without making it. I knew this was how she had left it on her last day, obviously unaware that she wouldn't be back to clean it up and certainly not knowing I would be traipsing through it.

I sat on the bed, feeling the softness of the quilt beneath me, breathing in her scent or at least what was left lingering. I looked around the room, seeing how little it had changed over the years. It was still the room I had shared a bed in, during those many sleepovers.

As I had gotten older, I had moved to my own bedroom down the hall, but I could remember the times I would come meet Dolores in her room and we would spend hours chatting, eventually falling asleep next to each other. She had been more than a simple grandmother to me, and as the memories flashed through my mind, I forced myself to step away from the deep chasm of sadness I felt approaching.

Downstairs, I heard something crash to the floor—something made of glass—and shatter. I cringed wondering what it could be and what idiot had broken it?

Walking to the window, I looked out over the orchards, to the lake below. Across the water, I could see my parents' house, all dark except for the small lights that lined the stairs to the veranda. No matter how I tried to stop it, the sight of the house brought back one specific memory from years before and soon, I was overtaken by it.

The bus dropped me off after school in the same spot it always did, but instead of walking home—the last place on earth I wanted to be—I turned in the opposite direction and walked toward my grandmother's home. Its white walls, its grey-tin roof, and red shutters all calling me to it. I walked across the wide, open yard, and knocked.

My grandmother opened the door, slightly surprised to find me there, but welcomed me in with a smile. Her house smelled of lilacs, apples, and cookies—always like cookies.

"Rough day?" she asked, seeing the tears pool in my eyes. I had managed to keep them at bay the entire ride home, but now in her presence, they were begging to spill over. "Come, let's have some tea."

She led me to the kitchen where she filled the kettle with water and placed it on the stove. I sat at the table, my head in my hands.

"It's so fucking awful, Grandma," I cried.

"Watch your language," she reproached me, walking over, placing her hand on my shoulder. "What's so awful?"

"Everyone is talking about it. I can't believe it," I said. "It's so embarrassing."

"Ellie, I can't exactly help you if you don't tell me what you're talking about," she said, walking back to the stove.

Removing the whistling kettle, she poured the water into two prepared teacups. I took a deep breath, preparing to confide in her. Surely she wouldn't like what I was about to tell her.

"I was in the cafeteria, talking with Brian and then Sabrina and Emilie walked over and said they'd seen Mom making out with Mr. Cormier, that fat real estate agent." I cringed just imagining my mom and him together. "I'm sure it's bull—sorry," I quickly corrected myself, my grandmother casting a warning glance. "But then Emilie said that everyone already knows about Mom and that she's having an affair!"

I looked at my grandmother, expecting her to console me, to tell me it was all nonsense but instead I found her eyes full of unwanted awareness and shame.

I felt the earth open up.

"It's not true, right? Please tell me it's just gossip."

"Elizabeth, listen," she began, but she didn't have to say anything else. Her hesitation told me everything I needed to know.

"Don't," I snapped, standing up abruptly. "How long have you known?"

"Not long."

"And why haven't you said anything?"

"It's none of my business. And it's none of yours. Your mother is an adult. She can make her own choices."

"So you're fine with her cheating on your son? How can you just let this happen?"

I looked out the window, at my house across the lake. I could imagine my dad coming home, wondering where I was. My mom would be home a little later. Would I tell her I knew? Would I make her tell my dad?

"Because you're upset, I'll forgive your rudeness," she said, putting me in my place.

"But Grandma, what am I supposed to do with this?"

"You're not supposed to do anything, Ellie," she was back at my side, handing me my cup of tea. Reluctantly, I took it but didn't drink. "You're still a child and this shouldn't have involved you. I am sorry you had to find out this way."

Tears ran down my face.

The sight of a few people running out of the house and into the trees below brought me back to reality, but my heartfelt stiff from the memory that still felt fresh.

My mother's affair had been the hardest thing I had ever gone through and the fact that my grandmother had known about it had only compounded that fact. Things weren't ever quite the same between us after that and the fights between my mother and I had only grown exponentially. My father had found out eventually—I had nearly forced my mother into telling him. They had fought, a lot. They had spent time apart. But even so, my father had eventually taken her back. They made up and now acted like the perfect couple.

I turned eighteen soon after my mother's infidelity and wasted no time in moving out. I couldn't stand her and the hurt she had caused him or me, for that matter. To make things worse, I couldn't stand my father for being so weak and for forgiving her so easily.

I started feeling that old, unresolved anger brewing and so I decided I needed some air.

Downstairs, the crowd had dispersed quite a bit, but without the buffer of the large crowd, I now felt out of place and conspicuous. My parents were sitting on the sofa, speaking with friends, but I felt absolutely no desire to join them. Weighing my options of either staying in the house making small talk with people I didn't even know or going for a walk outside, I chose the latter.

I stepped out into the crisp, clear night, and took a deep, cleansing breath. The stars were brighter than I had ever seen anywhere else, especially when compared to the city. The full moon cast such a bright light it almost felt as if it was daytime. I began to walk, realizing there was only one spot I truly wanted to be at that exact moment and headed through the orchard.

CHAPTER TWELVE

Reaching the bottom of the hill, I saw the fire pit off in the distance—a shoddy construction my grandparents and I had built over twenty years prior, but amazingly was still standing. At least twenty people could sit around the circular, brick and stone behemoth and not feel cramped. There had been no logical reason to make it so big, but as always, Dolores had gone ahead with one of my crazy ideas.

In all its existence I had never seen more than a dozen people sit in the surrounding chairs. Tonight, however, nearly every single chair was taken. I recognized several people from earlier, all sitting by the roaring fire, chatting.

A man was strumming a guitar and singing, flanked by a woman holding two toddlers. His name, Martin Lepage, popped into my mind as if it was yesterday. He had been our school's hockey team captain and one of Devon's best friends. I began to wonder if he was still as much of a prick as he had been in school. Arrogant, macho and rude, he was one of my least favourite people back then.

But now, while I watched him in the company of what appeared to be his wife and children, he seemed kind, pleasant, and the complete opposite of what I had known him to be. Maybe my preconceived notions were wrong and needed to be rethought. After all, if I had changed after so many years, or at least I thought I had, then wouldn't it be fair to assume he had too? The more I thought about it, the more I realized how all my long-held beliefs had been flipped on their heads over the past twenty-four hours.

Martin's voice was soft and melodic, bringing forth a surge of memories. I stared into the large bonfire, letting the past catch up with me. I was fifteen and I had gone to a party that Brian had dragged me to. Devon had been there, and I had been hopelessly in love with him. I could remember how it ended with me running home, crying. Every detail was clear as day, from the smell of the open field to the sound of Devon and Martin singing by the fire. I recalled the heat of embarrassment when Devon had spoken to me for the first time, and how I had been in such shock, I had stared at him, unable to speak. It had been my one chance to possibly be more than just his neighbour and instead, I had let my nerves get the best of me, ruining everything.

"A penny for your thoughts," Devon said, quickly bringing me back to the present.

"They don't make pennies anymore," I replied, grinning.

"Good point. Then a nickel?" he laughed, asking the man sitting next to me to give up his seat. "Or maybe I can offer you a S'more?"

Handing me a stick with a marshmallow hanging from its tip, Devon smiled, seeming pleased with the playful idea of making the messy campfire treat.

"I was just remembering that party at Jonathan Wilson's house. You and Martin had sung by the fire."

"Wilson had quite a few parties back then," he replied, unsure. "We usually ended up singing at most of them."

"Right. Forget it, it doesn't matter," I smiled shyly.

Devon had been a regular at those parties, whereas this specific one had been the only one I had ever been to.

"I never saw you there," he said a few moments later.

"They weren't really my thing," I dismissed, coolly. "And it's not like I would have been invited, anyhow."

"Why not? I don't think they required invitations."

He laughed and I supposed he was right. The parties, or so I had heard, had been a free for all when it came to the guest list.

"You know what I mean," I said. "I would have stuck out. I only went that night because Brian wanted to hook up with Jonathan."

A flicker of recollection lit up Devon's face.

"Was that the one where Brian and Jon were caught in the woods?"

That night had been quite a success in Brian's eyes, even though he had faced complete humiliation. He had managed to get some alone time with Jonathan, only to be caught, as Devon said, in the woods with his pants down. Everybody our age was buzzing that summer about the resident *gay kids* but all Brian cared about was finally having had a chance with his first serious crush since coming out.

"That's the one," I acknowledged, remembering how I had gone home by the time that had happened and I had missed all the fun.

"You didn't miss much. From the parties I can remember, they weren't that great. Kind of overrated."

"Of course you'd think that," I replied with a slight edge to my voice.

"What's that supposed to mean?" I hesitated, knowing Devon would see things differently and would probably laugh at me. "Come on, tell me," he urged.

His eyes peering into mine, having an unspeakable power over me, I gave in easily.

"You were one of the cool kids back then," I began. "Everyone loved you. You were popular, and that's fine, but I wasn't. I didn't spend my summers partying out there like you did. You were lucky to get to be part of that."

He laughed out loud, his laugh playful but drawing some attention, nonetheless. I felt my cheeks redden.

"Seriously? I think you're making it sound way more exclusive than it really was."

The way he had just brushed-off my opinion upset me a little, but it wasn't that surprising considering the alternate worlds we lived in back then.

"From your perspective, it must look like that," I said, a subtle hint of defensiveness to my words. "But I remember how it felt for me. That night was one of the best and worst nights of my life." I heard how it sounded once it left my mouth and immediately regretted it.

Why was I even getting into this now?

"How so?"

I let out a deep breath. "Those parties were infamous, but to get to go to one, well, that was amazing. And then there I was, sitting quietly by myself, absorbing the fact that I've been accepted into their inner circle, and who other than Devon Barrett sits next to me and starts to sing."

"Take it down a notch. You're making me sound like a fucking rock star."

I looked at him and wondered if the confidence I had always seen in him was a front. Maybe deep down, Devon had no idea just how perfect he was.

"That's how it felt for me," I said, without admitting my enormous crush on him. "I listened to you singing that night and I was in awe. And then…" I stopped, knowing I shouldn't continue.

"Then what?" His interest piqued.

I shook my head, regretting bringing it up. "Forget about it."

"No, come on, out with it."

"It's silly, really. You were about to talk to me and then Nicole jumped on you. You two started making out, and I felt humiliated and took off."

No sooner were the words out did I feel like a huge weight had been lifted. I could feel my cheeks flushing and my heart racing, but I finally felt free from the secret I had never told anyone before. I avoided looking up at him, staring deep in the fire instead, hoping we would move on as if I hadn't said anything. My fear was that I'd said too much and that he would now be uninterested in sticking around much longer.

"So you left the party because of *me*?"

His question surprised me. So did the fact that he looked genuinely worried that I had been hurt because of him.

"Well, not because of *you*, exactly," I replied, trying to soothe him. "I was a stupid teenager and..."

"And what?"

"And I had a hopeless crush on you," I admitted, shyly. "You know how it was back then, hormones and shit?"

I wanted to add that it had felt like more than a crush, that I was convinced I was in love with him, but I didn't. Nor did I add that seeing him with Nicole tonight had brought back all those unspoken feelings and I was now sitting with such wanting for him. No, I kept those thoughts to myself.

"I'm sorry," he said, his voice quiet. He leaned back in his chair. "I didn't know you felt that way."

"Don't be," I laughed, trying to play off the sudden seriousness between us. "It was a long time ago. And it was stupid."

"Please stop saying that. The last thing you are is stupid." I shrugged, thinking he was only trying to be nice. "No seriously, Elle. Don't say that. Sure, your reaction might have been a little extreme, but we've all had crazy reactions at some point or another."

"So, I'm not stupid, but I was crazy?" I teased.

"You know what I mean." He stopped, his thoughts clearly taking over that busy head of his. "It all makes sense, now. Why you were so distant with me all the time. Every time I saw you, you'd run the other way. I always assumed that you hated me or that I'd done something to piss you off."

"I never hated you, Devon," I said, blushing again. "It was just a bad crush."

"Well, it's too bad you never acted on it," he said, making me laugh hard.

From his look, I gathered he hadn't exactly been kidding.

I lifted an eyebrow. "As if you would have even seen me. You weren't exactly available."

"Ah, right, Nicole. We were pretty intense back then," he acknowledged. "Then again, you're pretty cute; I think I might have considered it. Had you given me the chance, that is. You avoided me like the plague."

I laughed along with him but was struck with regret. Had I not reacted so immaturely that night, if I had stuck around and been more confident, would things have gone differently? If I had stayed at the party, instead of running home, crying, would Devon and I have become friends, at the very least? Even the remote possibility that things may have gone differently between us made me feel uneasy.

"For what it's worth, I didn't think of you as the plague," I said. "But I guess we'll never know what might have been."

"Never say never," he said his tone light and flirtatious.

His focus was solely on me, a graham cracker in his hand. My marshmallow nicely roasted, I set it on the waiting cracker and the bed of chocolate, Devon setting the second cracker on top.

"You get the first bite." He held the sandwich out for me, his expression very suggestive.

Not sure how to eat it without it dripping all over my face, but not wanting to leave him hanging, I took a bite. As I did, Devon held my gaze, his eyes almost dancing with delight. I could feel the warm chocolate and marshmallow run down my chin and knew without a doubt, I had just proved there was absolutely no way to eat S'mores without looking like a five-year-old child.

Reaching into his shirt pocket, Devon pulled out and handed me a napkin, seeming unbothered by my sloppiness.

"Thanks," I said, wiping my chin. "I bet I look so attractive."

"Like you wouldn't believe." His voice oozed sexiness.

Was he flirting with me?

In an attempt to save face, I decided to play along and licked my lips in an oh-so-seductive way. I heard what sounded like a moan escape his mouth. Someone tapped him on the shoulder and offered him a joint. The strong, familiar smell had been lingering, but I had been too distracted to notice it headed our way. Devon took a few halls then handed it to me.

It had been years since I had smoked, but still feeling on edge from my day, I accepted. My lungs and throat burned at first, not used to the smoke, but after a few coughs, I could feel the buzz hitting me. Relaxation took over as I passed the joint along.

We both leaned back in our chairs and began to chat while sharing our snack. Every time he licked his lips I became aware of my growing desire for him. I didn't know if it was a side effect of the marijuana or if it was simply Devon's mere presence, but whatever it was, it was becoming incredibly difficult for me to ignore. His proximity, his demeanour, even the way he spoke to me in soft, gentle tones, made it hard for me to sit still. Desperately, I wanted to make a move. Even with everyone around to see it, I was just about to pounce on him, despite my better judgement.

"So, are you seeing anyone, Elle?" Devon asked. His question swiftly broke the spell he had me under.

I hesitated for a moment; just long enough to realize that I was, in fact, now single. The thought pleased me.

"No, not seeing anyone," I said, noticing a small, subtle smirk light up his face. "How about you? You and Nicole still seem pretty friendly."

Devon seemed taken aback, almost insulted.

"That's all we are, friends."

"Are you sure, because it didn't look like that," I said, forcing the topic a little further.

He sat straight up and pulled away from me. The change in his demeanour hit me hard, I felt a pang of disappointment, but I figured if it got the truth out of him, then it was for the best. Not that I was planning on acting on my feelings, but if I were to, I wouldn't want to be acting them out on someone who wasn't available.

"Yes. Just friends," he repeated a moment later. "Why, are you interested?"

I shook my head, seeing in his eyes that the wheels were

spinning.

"Just curious." I could tell he was searching for signs of my interest. "Brian mentioned you and Nicole being like *Ross and Rachel*."

"*Ross and Rachel?*" he laughed. "That's pretty funny."

I waited for him to say more on the subject. I knew it didn't really matter—or rather, that it shouldn't matter. Whether or not he was with Nicole should be of no concern to me. Whatever this feeling was that I had deep inside needed to subside and the more fuel I gave it by focusing on Devon, the worse it was getting.

He leaned in close and whispered, "Nicole is my past. It's as simple as that."

I smiled, despite myself, finding it hard to hide my relief. The way he looked at me gave me the impression I wasn't fooling him.

Someone in the group suggested we take our party into town, providing just the distraction I needed to get away from the topic at hand. Caught up in the nostalgia of the moment, truly enjoying myself for the first time in days, I accepted to go with them.

A part of me knew it was because the teenager in me was driving me to, but another part of me relished how being with them—and with Devon—kept my mind occupied on less important things. I felt free and unrestricted as if the act of being around these people gave me respite from the burdens I had been weighed down by.

Everyone walked up the hill, to where the cars were parked. Cramming as many people as possible into each vehicle, we headed down the dark, country road toward town.

I didn't know whose car I was in but I sat wedged in the backseat between Devon and some other guy, who was clearly high as a kite. He soon started talking my ear off about some nonsense. I nodded and tried to follow what he was saying, but I really wasn't too interested.

What had my attention, however, was the sudden pressure of Devon's hand on my thigh. He kept his eyes ahead but had a very knowing and naughty smile on his face. The guy next to me didn't seem to take notice and kept rambling on. I bit my lip and weighed my options, trying to come up with a reason to brush Devon's hand away. It struck me as very straightforward and brass of him to be touching me that way, but then again, it appealed to me.

Unable to convince myself otherwise—and maybe not wanting to truly find a valid reason to stop him—I let my body respond how it wanted to. I set my hand on his and gently moved it higher. I kept my eyes ahead as well, matching his conniving expression, but heard him clear his throat.

Oh, this was going to be a fun night.

CHAPTER THIRTEEN

The town's bar, affectionately named *Le Shack*, was situated in an old two-storey building. Upstairs were two rooms which gave it the qualification of a hotel, but calling it a hotel was being a little generous. It wasn't the classiest of places, and the rooms were generally used only by local patrons who had had one too many and needed a place to crash for the night.

Luckily for us, we were only there for the first floor.

We entered, Devon and I at the back of the group we had arrived with, and I could see the place was packed. I assumed this was due to the fact that in a town of fewer than three thousand residents, there wasn't much else to do on a Friday night. But the further we got the more I noticed that despite a few people sitting at the bar—regulars, I assumed—most of the people were the same I had seen earlier that evening at Dolores' wake. Behind the bar, hanging above the bottles of liquor, I spotted a large banner that read *We will miss you, Dolores!*

"What is this?" I asked, feeling a lump in my throat.

This wasn't just a spur-of-the-moment trip to the bar, as I had thought it was. Everyone here was here to honour my grandmother and despite the shabby locale, my heart filled with gratitude that so many people had come out to celebrate her life.

"You think she would have liked it?" Devon asked, quickly wrapping his arm around me with concern in his eyes.

At a loss for words, I just nodded and looked around. "Did you do this?"

"I had a part in it, sure," Devon squeezed me a little.

I was overwhelmed by his gesture. "I didn't realize she was so loved."

He smiled, "Honey, she was revered."

We approached the bar and while Devon ordered us drinks, I looked around the crowd. I could see Brian and Marc nearby, Brian was speaking to someone but was obviously looking at me, his expression full of wonder. I realized that what he was now seeing—Devon against me, his arm resting on my lower back—probably seemed surprising. I had to admit to myself that I would probably feel the same way had I seen this from the outside. Things were moving so fast, I was becoming so at ease with Devon, it didn't feel odd to have him touch me the way he had been doing.

Still, I shook my head ever so slightly at him, as if I was brushing off his assumptions. I certainly didn't want him—or anyone else—to get the wrong idea. Sure, there were flirtations, and I figured the weed had something to do with it, but there was nothing more between us.

Handing me my beer, Devon raised a toast to Dolores. Despite the number of people and the noise they created, the entire bar quieted down and joined in with a loud *Hurrah*.

I took a sip of my drink, trying to hide the uprising of sadness and spotted Nicole walking in. She saw Devon and walked directly toward us, as if on a mission. Before I knew what was happening, she had jumped onto Devon, wrapping her arms around his neck. Though barely noticeable to anyone but myself, she had very stealthily managed to pull him away from me and had now wedged herself between us. I stood, frozen and awkward. She had literally draped herself all over him and it was disgusting.

"I'm so happy you came!" she yelled, a little too loudly. "Isn't this great?"

Devon looked around and nodded. I could see him squirm a little but Nicole kept sinking her claws into him, not allowing him much wiggle room. It was clear he was being respectful but I really wanted him to tell her to leave.

Couldn't she see how uncomfortable she was making him?

"Come and dance with me," she urged, pulling on his arm. It was sad, desperate, really.

"No, thanks," Devon said, trying to be friendly about it but the annoyed look on his face was more than obvious. He gently removed Nicole's arms from his neck.

"What's wrong, 'D?'" she said, pushing her body against him. "Just one dance."

"Nicole, I said no," Devon snapped, sounding serious and to the point. Glad that he seemed genuinely irritated with Nicole, I found his severe tone incredibly sexy. "Now, if you don't mind, I'm going to go dance with her."

It took me a few seconds to realize he was talking about me, but by the time I had, he was wrapping his arm around my waist once more and leading me to the dance floor. Stunned, I followed him, feeling Nicole's glare on the back of my neck. When I turned to look in her direction, she seemed just as dumbfounded as I felt. It was like we were back to high school, at our yearly dances, when I would lean against the back wall, fantasizing that Devon would ask me to dance.

And now, here I was, dream becoming a reality and to top it off, he had just blown off Nicole. If it wasn't for that large banner at the bar reminding me of the reason why I was even here, I would have jumped for joy.

Devon led me through the crowd to the middle of the dance floor, though the name in itself was a great exaggeration when describing the ten-by-ten foot parquet floor. A few people were watching us, whispering to one another, trying to act like they weren't, and I could still feel Nicole's icy gaze from across the room. The last thing I wanted tonight was to have all eyes on me or be the centre of attention.

Now, that was precisely what I was. Devon stopped and wrapped his arms around my waist, drawing in my focus.

"I think Nicole might officially hate my guts now," I said, nervously.

"Well, we're not here for her, are we?" he said, pulling me against him, our hips joined.

It was clear I wasn't going to get away from Devon tonight and I wasn't entirely sure that was a bad thing. Sure, I felt guilty for the way he had blown off Nicole, but deep down, a bigger part of me was delirious at having one-upped her. It filled me with an unrecognizable confidence.

I wrapped my arms around Devon's neck, bringing him even closer to me. Soon, I lost all awareness of where we were and who was watching. I succumbed to my deeper senses and without words, I made it quite clear to Devon just how comfortable I felt with him. His hands were just below my hips as our bodies swayed side to side. I knew people were returning to their conversations, forgetting about the distraction that we had caused. Lost in my little world with my high school crush, I let the indescribable feeling overwhelm me.

He seemed just as entranced, his cheek resting against my head. Our body heat was climbing, my physical attraction to him increasing by the minute. I knew I should maybe take a break, distance myself a little bit, but I couldn't bring myself to do it.

Instead, as yet another song began, I held him closer still.

"Thirsty?" he suggested as if reading my thoughts. "That is if you want to stop dancing." He smiled at me, his eyes glowing and I knew he was teasing me. He held out his hand and we walked to a nearby table. "Here, sit. I'll be right back."

I watched him walk away, enjoying the view and was overcome by a sudden wave of fatigue. I'd been through quite a day and my earlier nap hadn't helped much. While Devon stood at the bar, casting occasional glances back at me, I became aware that I was now alone, with no one to use as a crutch. Devon was soon surrounded by his friends and seemed engulfed in whatever conversation they were now having. I knew the drinks would take a while, so I decided to head to the toilet.

Situated at the back of the bar, down a very dimly-lit hallway, I found the ladies room, which was nothing more than two stalls and one pedestal sink. As I washed my hands, I heard whoever had been in the neighbouring stall step out. I looked up to find a tall brunette standing over me. Even in the harsh neon light of the bathroom, Nicole looked like a supermodel.

"Oh, it's you," she said. She was trying to act surprised, but I could tell that she'd followed me in on purpose.

"Hi, Nicole," I said, drying my hands as quickly as I could.

"Listen, about you and Devon," she began.

"There's nothing between me and—,"

"Don't," she cut me off. Stepping closer to me, which was pretty close considering the size of the room we were in, she spoke, threateningly. "You can have your fun for the weekend, but you need to remember that he's mine. He's always been mine."

I was backing up a little, trying to avoid her warm breath on my face.

"Are you serious?" I started to hope someone would walk in and let me escape this awkward situation.

"Totally serious." She sneered at me, turning around and storming out.

Stunned, I leaned against the wall.

Had I travelled back in time?

We were in our thirties now, shouldn't this kind of behaviour be a thing of the past, reserved for teenage girls and their bullshit?

Stepping out of the room, I walked through the dance floor, crossing the crowd, keeping my eyes down. I avoided the bar, and Devon and his buddies, who were still laughing and chatting. I headed straight for the door.

I had barely reached it when I heard Devon shouting behind me.

"Elle! Elle, wait up." He caught up with me, grabbing my arm. "Where are you going?"

"I'm going home." I could feel the tears making their way up, desperate to spill over. "Thanks for tonight, but I really should leave."

"Really?" he asked, looking discouraged. "But we just got here. I thought we were having a good time."

I could feel the emotions taking their toll and I couldn't believe I was letting someone as horrible as Nicole get to me. Still, as I looked into Devon's eyes, I was filled with a sudden burst of frustration toward him.

"Be honest," I demanded. "You and Nicole aren't over, are you?"

"What makes you say that? Did she say something to you?"

He was looking behind him as if searching for her.

"It doesn't matter what she said. Answer me."

"As I told you before, we're just friends."

"Somehow I don't really believe that."

He shook his head and stepped closer to me.

"Well, we are. And I'm sorry you seem to have issues trusting people, but I'm telling you the truth."

"Right," I replied, doubtful.

"It's true. Despite what you think of me, I'm not a liar," he replied earnestly and reached for my hand. "Now, can you please come inside with me? I think you and I both deserve to have a good time, don't you?"

Though I was still annoyed as hell with Nicole and how she had made me feel—how she had brought up repressed anger I had felt decades ago—I also felt a little guilty leaving Devon high and dry. It was true that he had gone through the trouble of organizing this evening for my grandmother and the last thing I wanted was to give into Nicole and her childish ways.

I was stronger than that, wasn't I?

Before I could come to a decision, he began to lean in and my world stopped. All thoughts vanished as his lips touched mine, as his arms wrapped themselves around my waist. He stepped into me, his hips hard against mine and his tongue immediately found its way into my mouth. I let him kiss me, realizing I had never wanted anything more in my life. The kiss started softly, a little hesitant but built into something intensely passionate. I left my hands on his strong arms, gripping them so. A moan escaped my mouth as I kissed him harder.

Behind us, a large ruckus appeared out of thin air as a group of people walked out of the bar. It broke the spell between Devon and me, and we pulled apart. He smiled at me shyly, I could feel the heat in my cheeks, forcing myself to look away, slightly embarrassed by what had just happened.

"That was…" I giggled, unable to find the word.

"It really was," he agreed, his voice dripping with seduction.

Though his kiss had given me a brief reprieve from my reasons for wanting to leave, they soon came rushing back. However, now, considering what had just happened, I decided to go back inside and enjoy the rest of my night, maybe even rub it in Nicole's pretentious face. As improbable as the idea might have been a few days earlier, the prospect of hooking up with none other than Devon Barrett was now too good to pass up.

"Promise me one thing, though" I requested, as we headed back inside, my arm linked with his.

"Anything."

"Keep that fucking bitch away from me."

He laughed and wrapped his arm around me, "As long as you do the same for me."

Saturday, April 22nd

CHAPTER FOURTEEN

My temples were throbbing even before I managed to pull my eyes open. Strangely aware that I wasn't in my own bed, feeling the soft, foreign sheets against my skin, I looked around, trying to figure out exactly where I was. Snippets from the previous night were knocking at the exterior walls of my consciousness, trying to make their way in.

The room was bright, in a soft, glowing kind of way, but the sunlight hurt my eyes and compounded my headache. The king-sized bed I found myself in feeling like a vast expanse of cotton, and my legs were tangled in a large, white down comforter. To my left were immense, floor-to-ceiling windows, void of any curtains.

No curtains.

The realization hit me like a freight train.

I'm in Devon's bed!

I yanked the blanket up to my chin, suddenly mortified and fully aware of my near-naked state. I was wearing my bra and panties only, but could not for the life of me remember taking off the rest of my clothes. I couldn't remember sleeping with Devon and yet the evidence seemed to say otherwise. I thought back to the previous night, trying to make sense of my current predicament. The last thing I could recollect was taking several tequila shots at the bar following my encounter with Nicole.

Nicole.

She had made no further attempts to bother me, that much I could recall, and despite Devon's reassurances to the contrary, she still spent the night giving me horribly evil looks.

I remembered having been drunker than I normally would have been—probably due to the mix of marijuana and alcohol—and the nasty morning breath I could now taste told me I had definitely gone too far. From what I could recall, Devon and I had remained close, constantly touching or dancing, but there had been no more repetition of our kiss. I couldn't remember our night becoming anything more than that, but then again, as I now contemplated where I had woken up, maybe I was wrong.

No matter how hard I tried, I couldn't remember any more details. Not leaving the bar. Not coming back to Devon's house. And saddest of all, not sleeping with him. My inner teenager was yelling at me. My wish had finally come true and I'd been too wasted to enjoy it or have any memory of it.

Filled with disappointment, I crawled out of bed and cased the room for my clothes, holding my arm across my chest should he walk in and see me. I felt stupid. If we had, in fact, slept together, Devon seeing me in my panties would be old news. There really was no reason to hide my body, but still, I hurried around the room, modestly hunched over.

After searching through the impeccably clean room, and finding no trace of my clothes, I panicked. Whether or not we had slept together, there was just no way I could walk out of his bedroom half naked. Slipping into a plaid shirt I pulled out of his closet, which much to my relief covered my butt, I went looking for him, as well as some much-needed coffee. My head was absolutely killing. I hoped I would be able to get some aspirin to go along with some caffeine and definitely some answers about last night.

Being alone gave me the opportunity to see the inside of his house. I peeked quickly into the guest rooms as I walked by.

They were modern, very contemporary and clear of clutter—almost as if he didn't have company over very often. I had never been much of a fan of this particular style—having always considered myself a fan of the traditional builds—but I could see the beauty in its simplicity. I walked down the wooden staircase, with its glass and steel railing, and ended up in the kitchen, which opened up into a large space that included a small dining table and the living room. Devon was sitting at the table, sipping his coffee, wearing only a white t-shirt and some boxers.

Delectable, I thought as he looked up and smiled.

"Good morning, sweetness," he said, pouring me a cup of coffee. "Want some breakfast?"

I accepted, blushing and sitting down at the table, avoiding eye contact. He'd had as much to drink as I had the night before, maybe even more, yet he looked so unaffected by it. Surely he looked better than I did at that moment.

How was that possible?

In front of me, I found a plate of bacon, some croissants, and jam. Devon was rummaging through the refrigerator. I took a slice of bacon and immediately savoured its greasy goodness. As I buttered a croissant, I couldn't help but note how strange my current predicament felt and not just because my memories had been replaced by a gaping black hole.

"Scrambled eggs sound good?"

"Sure, I'll eat anything."

I watched him cook, humming a little tune, looking very happy. From my own personal experience, there was usually only one reason a man would be in such a good mood following a night like we'd had. I hoped I was wrong.

"Devon," I began, hugging my body as if to shield myself from the revelation that was about to come out. "Last night, did we…?"

Even though I knew I sounded prude, I couldn't bring myself to say the words, embarrassed as I was. He stood still for a moment, his back turned to me so I was unable to read his face. His silence and his sudden rigidity led me to believe that we had, in fact, slept together and that I had offended him by not being able to remember it. I had to admit that I would be pretty pissed if I was in his shoes.

Crap.

He took the frying pan off the burner and walked over to the table, filling my plate with eggs.

"Thank you," I offered, keeping my eyes down.

"As a matter of fact," he said after keeping me hanging for a few minutes. "The idea came to me several times last night, but sadly we didn't." He poured himself another cup of coffee and sat down across from me. "Call me old-fashioned, but when I sleep with someone I like them to be conscious for it."

The look he gave me was divine and made me swallow hard. Diverting my eyes again, I tried to hide the effect he was having on me but knew the colour in my face was giving me away.

"Besides," he continued. "We were way too wasted. It wouldn't have been how it could be."

"How it *could* be?" I choked a little on my eggs.

He grinned mischievously. If I didn't know any better, I would have said he was incredibly pleased with his air of mystery.

"Do you have any plans today?" I asked in an effort to change the subject.

"That depends on what your plans are. I was thinking we could hang out," he said. "If you feel up to it, that is." He let out his small laugh that told me he was teasing.

The same giddiness I had felt the previous evening rushed over me once more.

What was it about him that made me feel like this?

I knew my time would be better spent focusing on the recent upheaval of my life that was looming over my head but at that exact moment, hangover or not, there was nothing I felt like doing more than spending the day with Devon. Just the idea of it was intoxicating.

I glanced out of the panoramic windows, at the lake and could see the sun shining, the trees swaying ever so softly, hinting that there was the lightest of breezes. I could already sense the warm, comfortable spring day and knew it was my favourite kind of weather—not too warm, not too cold, just a gentle crispness in the air. It was the kind of day that always made me want to be outside. At that moment something helped me decide—I could deal with life and its bullshit later.

"What did you have in mind?"

My heart fluttered as Devon stepped behind me, putting his hands on my shoulders, squeezing gently.

"First off," he leaned down, whispering in my ear, his lips brushing against my skin. "Let's take a shower." I looked up at him, unable to hide my surprise. "Separate showers," he clarified.

Strangely, as nervous as I had been waking up naked in his bed, I was now a little disappointed at not being able to take a shower with him. I let the picture of him showering take over my thoughts. I could imagine the water running down his tanned skin, down his stomach, his legs. I could picture each muscle, wet and warm. The thought made my thighs tighten and I desperately wanted to see more, but couldn't bring myself to take it any further.

"And after showering?" I asked, barely able to stop my voice from quivering.

"That part is a surprise." He was being a tease, but I didn't mind.

I entered the long, galley-style bathroom. It was decorated with slate tiled floors, black cabinets and a large skylight above filled the room with light. At the back, located behind a glass wall was the bathtub and shower sitting on a floor made up of beautiful pebble stones in varying shades of grey and blue. There was something very serene and tranquil about it all.

I let the water from the rain shower-head rush over me, feeling it relieve my lingering hangover. As I worked the ultra-creamy body wash into a lather, recognizing Devon's scent immediately, I came to the realization that I still had no idea where my clothes were.

Once I was done, I wrapped myself in a large, thick white

towel and smiled at the absurdity of my dilemma. Things could definitely be worse than wondering where my clothes were while I was naked in Devon Barrett's shower! As if he had read my mind, Devon was waiting outside the room holding a neatly folded pile of clothes.

"I washed them this morning," he said, handing them over. "I hope you don't mind."

"Mind?" I laughed, thanking him. "You cook and do laundry? Is there anything you don't do?"

"Very little," he joked and went for his shower.

I fought back the urge to open the door and peek at him naked. The fact that the only thing standing between me and him was a very skinny wooden door, made the temptation that much greater and harder to resist.

I pulled myself together, wondering where these impulses were coming from and walked back to his bedroom. Reluctant to wear the same thing I had worn the previous day, I improvised and kept Devon's shirt instead of my own. I hoped he wouldn't mind. Besides, as I looked at myself in the mirror, paired with my jeans, his checkered shirt actually looked good on me. Devon was still in the shower when I came back downstairs, so I went to wait outside by his Range Rover.

I felt minuscule next to the car. It was a nice vehicle, to be sure. Maybe *nice* wasn't the right word. It was large, sleek and the most interesting colour—a sort of black with blue undertones. I tried to peek inside, but the windows were fairly well-tinted and I couldn't see much. And so I leaned against the car, hoping not to trigger his car alarm—assuming he had one—and waited.

I was now all alone with nothing but the thoughts running through my head. Taking a moment to think, I went over what had happened the previous night or at least what I could remember of it, and what I had found out this morning.

I had never spent such a night with anyone before. Even when things were good with Paul he had never shown me such a good time. Then again, maybe it wasn't Paul the issue, maybe it was just that I had never felt for him what I now felt for

Devon.

I looked up at the sky and took a deep breath.

How did I let myself get here?

My efforts to fight these feelings had been futile and now I was spending the day with him despite knowing I should be doing the exact opposite and distancing myself. I had more important things to worry about.

Devon emerged, dressed in a white, v-neck t-shirt paired with a pair of slightly loose, well-worn jeans. His eyes were hidden behind a pair of black Ray-Ban sunglasses and the baseball cap on his head was backward. He looked so young and carefree yet still incredibly sexy. He grinned at me, in that oh-so-mischievous way that yet again made my knees quiver. He clearly hadn't taken the time to shave, his face scruffy, but I didn't mind. It looked great on him.

"So where are we headed?" I asked. He shook his head as he approached me. "You won't even give me a little hint?"

"Trust me, it'll be worth it." He winked and held the door open for me.

I thought about it and realized that strangely, I did trust him. I didn't know much about him—nothing, really, other than what he had told me the day before—but something about him made me feel like I could trust him with my life.

I had never known anyone who made me feel so untroubled, so safe. I became filled with uncertainty at the thought but also strangely invigorated, too.

CHAPTER FIFTEEN

We hadn't been in the car for very long before Devon pulled into the small parking lot. We were a few feet from my grandmother's house—mine now, I reminded myself—and I barely recognized the building that held the offices of the *Williams' Family Orchards* company. It used to be my grandmother's neighbour and someone's home. She had bought it years ago and had converted over the years. Now, it was a fully operational, two-storey building that housed the sales, marketing, and other operational offices.

Though at first glance the building looked like your run-of-the-mill farmhouse, very rustic and quaint, the business run within its walls ran like a well-oiled machine. The orchard's products ranged from basic apple products, which were distributed to local stores all the way to award-winning ciders that were sold throughout North America and even in some parts of Europe. I had always been impressed by how well Dolores had managed the business in such a competitive market, and now with her gone, I felt ashamed for never having fully expressed that to her.

We went inside and were welcomed by an older lady who was sitting at the reception desk. Genevieve—or Gigi, as she insisted on being called—smiled and put the phone down.

"Elizabeth!" she said, walking over and taking me in her arms. I had hardly recognized her, she had changed quite a bit since the last time I had been there. "How are you? No, that's a silly question, I'm so sorry. Things just aren't the same without her here."

She looked down and I could tell she missed my grandmother immensely. Gigi had worked at the orchards for most of my life and I couldn't remember a time when she hadn't been part of it.

Her eyes filled with tears and I took her hand. "You're right, but you know she'd tell us to move on."

She smiled, taking a tissue from her desk and blowing her nose, "That's true, she would."

"I'm going to show Elizabeth around, alright Gigi?"

She nodded and returned to her desk as Devon led me away, down the hall. We walked by converted cozy little offices that had once been bedrooms and I saw a few employees who seemed very busy. It was rather quiet and then I remembered it was Saturday. The fact that anyone was at work when they should be relaxing at home was a surprise, but then it wasn't uncommon, knowing how busy they got in the spring. Devon explained that now was when all the orders came in and when their sales were the highest. I took in the information and made a note of it, seeing as it would appear it was now my responsibility to know such things.

We rounded a corner and walked through a wooden door.

"This is my office," Devon said, grinning with pride like a kid showing off his new toy.

The room was light and airy, the walls decorated with artwork and books. It resembled someone's personal study more than an office.

"Nice digs you have here," I said, walking to the bookcase. It was filled with dozens of books, from classics to ones about business and economics.

"Thanks," he said. "Want a drink? Coffee, water?"

"Coffee sounds great," I replied.

Devon walked to a small counter near his desk, set up with

a single-cup coffee machine and some bottled water. I watched him prepare my drink. His hands looked so powerful, so strong, I found that just the sight of them took my breath away. Even the nape of his neck where his hair was closely shaved made my insides tighten. It dawned on me that this might be the surprise he had mentioned earlier but I certainly hoped it wasn't. Sure, I appreciated seeing his office, and all the renovations that had been done in recent years, but it wasn't what I thought he had in mind when he had mentioned it at breakfast. I was growing a little disappointed, thinking it might be all he had in store.

"Here you are," he said, handing me my cup, snapping me out of my thoughts.

I thanked him and sat down in the small sitting area situated by the window that looked out on the orchard. He sat across from me and crossed one leg over the other.

"The place looks like it's running well," I said, aiming for business talk. "It was nice seeing Gigi. I'm happy she's still here. It's like having a little bit of my grandmother."

We smiled together.

"She's terrific. She's planning on retiring next year, though. Not sure what we'll do without her."

"That's too bad," I replied, genuinely sad. "I'm sure you'll find someone."

"We will." His eyebrow arched up. "We're not really going to talk business today, are we?"

"You're the one who brought me here. If not for business, then for what?"

He stared into my eyes and I could feel my heart thump. My breathing accelerated in response to the simmering excitement below the surface.

He grinned and stood up. "Come. I want to show you something."

We left his office and walked down the hallway to a large room. A light, fragrant smell surrounded me as we walked in. It was apparent it was for meetings and such since there were several chairs set up around a long table. However, it wasn't cold and sterile like most conference rooms usually were. This one seemed warm, welcoming. The table was a very long slab of wood that Devon explained had been cut from a single tree. The piece was at least twelve feet long and was polished in a way that beautifully enhanced each knot and its grain. There were dozens of plants throughout the room, some suspended from the ceiling, some on pedestals. Along the back wall was a large projection screen, which really was the only modern element that broke the otherwise natural and calm decor.

"I wanted you to see these," Devon said, pointing to some pictures on the walls.

I stepped closer to look at them and realized they were of past office parties and different company functions. More importantly, I found my grandmother in every single one, smiling with pride, her arms around her employees as if they were family.

I walked around the room, looking at each black and white portrait, amazed at the time span they covered. The first one, by the door, was a picture of my grandparents in front of their house circa nineteen-forty-nine—my grandmother beaming and pregnant. The pictures continued through the years, the final one as recent as this past Christmas. It warmed my heart to know she had always been present in the company's day-to-day and had been so close to her employees.

"These are amazing, Devon," I said, my voice soft. "Really beautiful."

"They are. I prefer being in this room than my office sometimes," he admitted, standing close to me. "It makes me feel like—,"

"Like you're home," I answered, certain I knew what he was going to say.

"Exactly."

I didn't look directly at him but could feel his eyes on me.

"I think I understand why you showed me this today."

"You do?"

"I get it, I do. This place, what it means to everyone. What it meant to her," I smiled at my grandmother's face, feeling like she was looking right at me. "It helps a little, I suppose."

"I hope it does. I just wanted you to see that you've inherited a family here, not just a business," he said, warmly.

His eyes were full of love and admiration, and I was suddenly struck with such sadness as if the last few days had caught up with me and the finality of my grandmother's passing now felt brutally real. I hadn't even noticed I was crying until Devon stepped closer to wipe my tears away.

"Don't cry," he said, lifting my chin. "I didn't mean to make you sad."

"It's fine," I said, dismissively. "I just miss her. I guess it hasn't hit me yet. Or it just did."

He pulled me into a hug and I pressed my face against his chest. His hand stroked my back, up and down and I felt overcome with a feeling of comfort.

"Come, let's get out of here," he proposed, taking me by the hand and leading the way.

I followed him willingly, knowing there was no point in asking him where he was taking me.

CHAPTER SIXTEEN

We drove out of town, my mind lost in thought. I had been so busy thinking back on the images Devon had shown me in the office that I had hardly paid any attention to where we were going. When I looked out the window, even though I was fully intent on figuring it out, I definitely could not recognize the area. Even if I asked, I knew he wouldn't tell me, so instead, I tried to press him for advice.

"If you were me, would you keep it all?"

"The orchards?" He glanced at me and I could tell he saw that there was plenty of doubt in my mind. I saw him crease his eyebrows, giving it some thought. "Well, I can't really answer that, Elle. I'm not you."

"I understand that, but humour me." I didn't know why, but I felt his opinion would actually help me in some way. "If you were in my shoes, what would you do?"

He took a deep breath as we turned onto a dirt road. I looked up ahead, still unable to tell where we were going.

"I guess I'd try to run it as well as Dolores did and try to make her proud." His answer filled me with trepidation and he smiled as if seeing the worry on my face. "Don't worry, Elle. Do your best and I'm sure it will all work out."

"That's the thing, though. I don't know the first thing

about running a company." I let out a long sigh, feeling exasperated. "I'm sorry. I guess I'm not being very good company."

He reached over and gently squeezed my thigh. The act caught me by surprise but I didn't dare move.

"I'm sure Dolores didn't expect you to know everything right from the get-go."

My grandmother had been clear in her suggestion that I speak with Henri should I have any questions, but nowhere had she mentioned who to talk to for guidance about running a highly successful business.

"You'll do fine."

"And you'll be there for me?" I could hear the open meaning within my question, which wasn't at all how I had intended it to come out. "I mean if I have questions or whatever?" I replied quickly, unsure if I had been able to hide my blunder.

"If you need help, I'm here for you, anytime." The car took yet another turn. "You need to understand, though, that it's a lot of work. Busy days, nights, even weekends. Not much time to relax, but when all is said and done, it's worth it." He looked at me, and I could tell he felt my anxiety. "But I'm biased, it doesn't really feel like work for me, you know?"

He searched my eyes for some understanding. I wanted to smile in recognition, but the reality was that I couldn't.

I had no idea what he meant. I had never thought of work as anything but just that: work. Though I had dreamt of one day having a job that I loved, the truth was I had not found it yet. I hoped he wouldn't press the subject because I didn't feel like admitting my entire life's plan had crumbled and I was now just working to pay the bills.

I knew he loved his job, and I appreciated his passion for it, but I knew that I would probably never feel the same as he did about the orchards. It now represented so much loss to me—both my grandparents were attached to it and were gone—and I would never be able to immerse myself in it the way they all had.

The car slowed down as we made our way down a small, country road. Our destination came into view as we passed under a large, iron archway that read *Les Écuries Gallant*.

"Oh, no, you're kidding. We're going horseback riding?"

"You're not scared of horses, are you?" he asked, parking the car.

"Maybe you should have asked me that before we got here?" I joked but still felt a little nervous as we got out of the car. I waited while Devon fished a backpack out of the trunk and then followed him to the main building.

"If you don't want to, I'll understand."

"It's not that. I've just never done it before."

"Never?" he asked, his surprise obvious. Opening the door for me, he leaned in and said, "Don't worry, I'll keep you safe."

He gently stroked my cheek with his thumb, filling me with a feeling of serenity and for some reason, I couldn't quite understand, I felt yet again like I was in safe hands.

We walked into the ranch's office and were met by an older man with white hair and the most enchanting smile. He introduced himself as Robert Gallant, but he insisted I call him Bob. Soon, I could see the ease and familiarity between him and Devon. They started speaking to each other, sharing small talk and the easygoing way they spoke to one another confirmed that they had known each other for quite a while.

Bob offered me his condolences. "Dolores and I have been friends for a long time," he explained, then corrected himself. "*Were* friends."

His big, blue eyes filled with tears and I got the distinct impression that his relationship with Dolores may have been more than platonic.

Though my grandfather had died nearly twenty years before, I had never given much thought to my grandmother's love life after he had passed. Bob was a fairly handsome man and I realized that it wasn't entirely that far-fetched to imagine him dating Dolores. After all, as I was slowly learning every minute I spent in my hometown, there was a lot my grandmother had kept to herself.

Guiding us out to the paddocks, Bob introduced us to our riding companions for the day. The first horse was named Sunshine. He was a small, black gelding that seemed to fit his name perfectly, exuding warmth and letting me stroke his muzzle.

His neighbour, on the other hand, was a horse named Lucky. She was an enormous brown mare, who seemed feisty and independent. I got the impression that her name was indicative of how one would feel if they came back alive after riding her. She was so full of energy that even Bob, who was definitely a well-seasoned rider, was having difficulty reining her in.

As if sensing my anxiety, Devon leaned over and whispered, "Don't worry, she's mine."

Though I wasn't entirely relieved that Devon would be taking a chance with Lucky, I was, in all honesty, thankful I wasn't going to be the one riding her. With the horses saddled and ready to go, Devon helped me up onto Sunshine. The horse felt gigantic to me, even though Bob told me that he was one of his smallest horses.

"He's a sweetheart," Bob reassured me, handing me the reins, explaining the commands I needed to know. Sunshine remained still and relaxed, easing my jitters.

Devon double checked all the equipment, walking around my horse, pulling on straps and other things, making sure I was comfortable.

"We don't have to do this if you don't want to," he reminded me, looking empathetic. Again, he placed his hand on my thigh, sending shivers through me, immediately calming my worries.

"Let's do it," I said, cringing at my choice of words.

Why did his touch make me so nervous?

He nodded, unphased by what I said and approached Lucky. She fussed and seemed a little hesitant at first, but Devon took her face in his hands and whispered something in her ear. She soon calmed down and even nuzzled up to him.

I looked on, amazed.

"It's unbelievable how good he is with that horse," Bob said, standing by me. "He's the only one that can ride her, you know? But then again, they're always better with their owners aren't they?"

"Owner?" I asked, my eyes wide with surprise.

"Ready?" Devon asked before Bob could respond.

I nodded. Devon beamed, his face alight with a truly genuine and contented smile.

So Devon Barrett owns a horse?

I shook my head in disbelief. Here I was assuming these horses belonged to the ranch, not once even considering the possibility that Devon might own one. It seemed there was much more to him than I had previously gleaned.

He led the way out of the paddock, down a dirt path that disappeared into the woods beyond. I followed behind him, still feeling slightly unsure on the tall horse, but also feeling such a high level of excitement for what might possibly be coming around the bend.

CHAPTER SEVENTEEN

We strolled through a tunnel of birch trees, their green leaves shimmering in the late morning's sun. I was starting to get the hang of riding—Sunshine and I slowly developing a rhythm. He kept his pace to a trot, as I tried desperately to keep my balance and not fall off.

Soon, the path widened and Devon slowed down, guiding his horse to my side.

"See, you're a natural. Nothing to worry about," he said, his smile reassuring me if only a little bit.

"How long is this trail anyhow?" I didn't want the ride to end necessarily, but my lower body craved some rest.

"The entire trail? About ten kilometres," he said, smiling. My eyes popped out of my head, making him laugh out loud. "Don't worry, we'll be stopping soon."

A few moments later, he slowed down and took a right turn through some bushes. I followed suit. We went down an even smaller, almost inconspicuous path. This clearly wasn't his first time here—the path would only be known to a habitual rider. I would have walked right by it. Within moments, we had reached an idyllic grassy clearing interspersed with weeping willow trees and a small brook.

I followed Devon toward the water, where he tied our

horses' reins to a nearby tree, letting them graze and drink. He helped me dismount, placing his hands on my waist, lifting me down from the stirrups without any difficulty.

With his bag in his hands, he walked to one of the weeping willows and took out a large, plaid blanket. I helped him lay it down on the ground, under the shade of the tree. Though summer was still quite a while away, the day had become exceptionally warm.

We sat down. Devon reached into the bag, taking out several containers. I opened one to find various fruits and vegetables. In another were some cheese and crackers. Unsure when he'd had the time to get everything ready, I glanced up at him, impressed.

"You really come prepared, don't you?" I said, popping a piece of cheese into my mouth.

"I used to be a boy scout," he laughed. "It's mandatory."

I wasn't sure if he was being serious, but I could imagine him as the leader, guiding his fellow scouts, teaching them how to camp and make fires using nothing but some sticks and a rope. The thought made me smile.

We ate quietly, Devon looking at the creek, pensive. I knew then that my opinion of him had been turned completely on its head in the last two days. I watched him appreciating the beauty of our surroundings and though the day had been great so far, I was curious as to what exactly he might be expecting and worried that this might lead to something more serious, something I wasn't entirely sure was a good idea.

"Devon," I said, clearing my throat. "Why did you do all of this?"

He looked at me as if my question didn't make sense.

"I wanted to spend time with you. Maybe take your mind off things." I bit my lip, considering his answer. "You don't like it?"

"I do," I answered swiftly, seeing the expectation in his eyes. I was grateful for the distraction, even if I was uncertain where it would lead. "It all just seems a little romantic."

"And you don't do *romantic*?" he asked, his eyes suggestive but soft.

I blushed and forced myself to look away. The fact was that from the moment I woke up until this very second, the day had been perfect—something I could only have dreamt of. And even then, not even my subconscious could have come up with something as pleasant.

But as I took in his deeply serious expression, and as his insanely captivating eyes peered into mine, I had to face the reality that I did do romantic and that I wanted it, desperately. Paul had never been one to shower me with anything more than very rare expressions of love and maybe occasional gifts. I suppose I had grown accustomed to it being that way and had never stopped to question what I was missing or what I needed from my relationships.

Now that I found myself with someone I was deeply attracted to and who was putting in the actual effort to show me a good time, it made me unsure how to proceed. Was this all a glimpse of what it could be like between Devon and I or was he only putting on a show to get me to sleep with him? I remembered the supposed on-and-off relationship he had with Nicole. It wasn't too far-fetched of an idea to think that Devon might just be looking for a fling, taking advantage of the fact that I wouldn't be sticking around for much longer. Taking advantage of my vulnerability.

And to make matters worse, I felt like I couldn't get a grip on my feelings. I was all over the place, no matter how Devon was making me feel deep inside. I felt like I couldn't be sure if I was following my heart or just hiding behind the distraction he was offering.

And how that distraction was enticing.

"You didn't have to do all of this," I said, the words sounding far more pathetic than I had intended them to. "I don't want you getting the wrong idea."

He let out a long sigh but didn't seem annoyed.

"First of all," he answered, inching closer. "I was going to take Lucky out for a ride today, anyhow, so it wasn't that much trouble having you tag along."

He reached into a container and took out a strawberry. Holding it by the stem, he rolled it between his index and thumb, making me swallow hard. There was something deeply seductive in the way he was holding it—the way his fingers, so strong and long, were handling the soft, red fruit.

"Secondly," he continued, leaning into me, lifting the strawberry as if he was about to feed it to me. "I'm not getting the wrong idea. I really like you, Elle, and I like spending time with you."

Gently, he ran the strawberry along my lips. Initially, his straightforwardness stunned me, even though I quickly reminded myself that it shouldn't. Devon had made more than one or two moves lately and it really wasn't a surprise where this was headed. I was nervous, felt my heartbeat quicken, but my desires took over and I went along with it, throwing all hesitations to the wind.

Grinning, I took a bite of the fruit, while gazing deep into his eyes. He smiled. I licked my lips ever so slowly, making him bite his lower lip. Suddenly, I became acutely aware of our breathing, no longer hearing the sounds around us. I didn't care that we were outdoors—we could have been in the middle of a crowded park and I would have had the same reaction. Captivated by our surroundings, I surrendered to my hunger.

I reached for him, pulling him down on top of me. His lips were on mine instantly, his kiss intense and consuming, taking my breath away. His tongue found mine and I felt his thigh in between my legs. His weight pressed down on me, making me feel safe and I forgot all the reasons why I should stop what was about to happen.

Devon pulled back, removing my pants. Never dropping his gaze, he lowered himself again and kissed my legs and the insides of my thighs. My body arched up in response. I watched, propped up on my elbows, as he wet his finger and gently inserted it into me. The feeling was mind-blowing. His touch, warm and soft, yet also strong, almost immediately made me come undone. He moved in and out with increasing speed, all the while planting soft kisses on my thighs, making me moan a little louder than I had meant to. With his other hand, he began to rub me in just the right spot, bringing me closer and closer to the edge of my orgasm. I writhed with pleasure, pushing against his hand, giving myself that little extra satisfaction.

Suddenly, he stopped and was on top of me again.

"Elle," he said, his thigh taking over where his hands had just been. "Can I fuck you now?"

"Yes, but I'd like to see you naked first," I said, reaching for him and unzipping his jeans, making him smile with what seemed like self-satisfaction. He looked up at me as if baffled. "Properly, this time, and not through a window," I added, not about to give in without seeing him in all his glory. In truth, I was a little stunned at my own bluntness but I knew I owed my inner-teenager for messing up last night.

He surrendered, laughing and stood up. His shirt came off first, revealing the same muscular body I had remembered from high school, but now with that added definition of a grown man. Those few, curvy teenage pounds had been replaced by lean, sculpted muscles. His skin was still the same caramel colour I'd been obsessed with. He reached for his pants, but I stopped him.

"Wait! Slowly," I commanded. I wanted to enjoy every second of this.

"You're a little pervert, aren't you?" he joked, returning to the task at hand.

As slowly as I was sure his body would allow him, he removed his jeans. He was wearing grey boxer-briefs, but not for long. He stepped out of them and revealed himself to me. He stood, glaring at me as if waiting for the word *Go*.

I took in the view. I had never given much thought to what my ideal man should look like, but at that moment, I realized he was its personification. He had a washboard stomach, his waist the perfect width, all leading to that v-shape—what I had always called the *road to riches*. I stared, surprised by his considerable endowment.

Perfection.

"Uncomfortable?" I asked, noticing him squirm a little.

"Not in the least. I'm an exhibitionist, remember?" he replied, fully confident. He nodded in my direction. "Quid pro quo. Your turn."

I pursed my lips but accepted his challenge, seeing as I was already halfway there. I sat up and started to remove my shirt.

"No, no, no," he interrupted. "Stand up."

I stood, feeling incredibly exposed. His gaze grew hotter and he licked his lips. I obeyed, removing my panties, then bra, suddenly very aware that I was outdoors.

He stepped closer to me, brushing his hand along my stomach and around to my back. Grabbing my ass firmly, he pulled me against him, our hips colliding. His lips were on my neck as he swiftly lifted me off the ground. I wrapped my legs around his waist, running my fingers through his hair. He knelt back down on the blanket, settling me on his lap. I pressed my weight down on him, feeling him beneath me and moved ever so slightly, hearing him moan. The sound was music to my ears. With one arm he reached into his bag and pulled out a condom.

"Always prepared," I joked, nibbling his earlobe.

He leaned into me, pushing me onto my back.

"Always," he smiled, ripping the foil packet and rolling the condom on.

The seconds felt like hours, my desire difficult to contain. He lowered himself, his elbows on each side of my head. Looking deep into his eyes, I returned his smile as he entered me with one swift push.

He stilled as if savouring the moment. I could feel him tense a little more as he pulled out slowly, only to return with another hard thrust. It wasn't painful, not in the least. I matched each powerful thrust with my own, letting my accumulated and unsatisfied feelings of the past few days take over. His momentum quickened, still thrusting hard, but moving faster and faster.

Our combined screams and moans echoed in the open meadow, as we grew unconcerned with being heard. The soft springtime breeze caressed our exposed skin and my body became more and more sensitive. My orgasm grew in a way I had never experienced before. I felt like I wanted the experience to last forever; to have him in me for as long as possible—to make time stand still. Yet, my need for release was becoming too difficult to control. I sensed it was the same for him, his moans becoming more and more arduous.

Unable to keep holding on, I let go, all my muscles tensing and quivering, my skin overcome by goosebumps. As I tightened around him, Devon gave one more strong push and came as well, pressing his body onto mine. His weight was crushing but the feeling of his skin's warmth against mine made my orgasm that much more intense. Reaching our full release, our breathing steadied and became synchronized. The lull of his breathing flooded me with a wave of fatigue.

Devon kissed my forehead, my cheeks, my neck, and relaxing his body against mine, he placed one hand on my breast. His fingers caressed and tickled my skin. The affection was welcomed, as I ran my fingers up and down his back. We let our bodies relax, and coming down from my high, I began to shiver a little.

"Are you cold?" Reaching around me, he took the blanket and wrapped it over me.

"Thanks."

The intensity of the moment started to wean and I was growing more and more aware of my nudity. I felt a growing shyness creeping in. Devon was cuddling up to me, holding me in his arms, but all I could do was look up into the blue sky, watch the clouds roll by, and begin let my worries take over.

"That was..."

"Yeah, it was," he replied.

"How do you know what I was going to say?" I turned my body to him, his belly against mine.

"I guess I don't," he answered, pulling me closer still.

My lips against his chest, I smiled, kissing him. I could lay like this forever, I thought, shocked by how I felt. I had barely been too keen on sleeping with Devon a few hours ago and now after having sex with him only once I was ready to stay with him forever? I assumed it was yet another side effect of my lingering teenage angst and dismissed the thought from my mind.

This would not turn into something long-term, I reminded myself. *It could not.*

"Maybe we should get going?" I asked, abruptly, surprising even myself.

I felt him stiffen next to me. "We just got here. And the food..."

I sat up and looked at the containers that were now knocked over, food spilled on to the grass. There was something within me, greater than me, that was panicking. Now that my mind had been freed from unexplored desires, my nerves were clearly taking over and doubt was starting to simmer. Common sense made me wonder if I had just made a huge mistake. This entire weekend's weight had shifted from one problem to a completely new one, and now it felt as if it was crushing me.

"I'm really not that hungry." I knew very well that I was being rude and in truth I was famished.

"You're not?" He didn't seem too convinced.

I shook my head. "I appreciate all of this, but I think I should get home."

"If that's really what you want."

He stood up, handing me my shirt, which I put on hastily. As quickly as I was getting dressed, he did the opposite, taking his time. I could see he was upset, avoiding eye contact and I was soon overcome by guilt. A flash of doubt passed through me, and I could hear my inner-teenager screaming *You moron!*

Thoughts of Paul, of my grandmother, and especially of the Orchard overwhelmed me and I felt as if they were starting to suffocate me. I knew I couldn't handle even one more complication, and despite my intense attraction to him, Devon was becoming exactly that—a complication.

We walked back to the horses, which were still grazing quietly by the river and I waited while Devon tied the bag to

Lucky's saddle. I felt like I should say something, but instead, not able to come up with anything remotely helpful in this situation, I remained silent. I could see his frustration simmering below his otherwise calm surface and assumed talking would only lead to a fight—and I definitely wasn't interested in a confrontation.

I got back in Sunshine's saddle, this time unassisted by Devon, who seemed too preoccupied with his horse, and I felt sad and frustrated. If only I had stuck to my original gut feeling and had kept things platonic, he and I might not be in this awkward place.

Soon we were back on the path, leaving our little sanctuary behind. I became convinced that he was going to give me the silent treatment all the way back home. The ride to the paddock, which had seemed long on our way in, now seemed like it would take an eternity.

CHAPTER EIGHTEEN

Once we had returned the horses to the stables, Bob wished us a good day. Devon and I were polite, but I could see in the old man's eyes that he could tell something had changed between the both of us. He smiled at me, almost knowingly and it took all my strength to return the smile.

In the car, the awkwardness was becoming unbearable and I felt like I had to speak up, but Devon beat me to it.

"Listen," he said, as we pulled out onto the main road. "I'm sorry if this felt rushed. I just wanted to show you a good time. Get your mind off things."

His eyes searched mine and I could feel my heart wanting to leap out of my chest. Sure, I could admit how amazing it all was and then see where it could lead. And I could assume that I would never get tired of it, but that didn't mean that he wouldn't. Who was I kidding? There was no way a man like him would want a girl like me, at least not long-term. Us being together was too complicated, anyhow, not to mention completely unfathomable.

"You don't regret it, do you?"

I sighed, unsure how to explain what I was thinking but feeling like I was suddenly trapped. I needed to get out of this situation, to get away from him, if only to clear my mind and figure everything out.

"No, not exactly. It was great. You were great." I was nervous as hell and starting to stutter. "I just don't think this was a good idea."

He remained quiet, his silence making me even more nervous.

"I'm sorry, Devon. I can't see this going anywhere."

There, it was out, I thought, half relieved.

"Right," was all he said.

I watched him, gauging if he was going to say anything else. Instead, he stared at the road ahead. I sighed, feeling drained and looked out the window, trying to ignore the feeling of defeat growing inside.

"Why exactly do you think this needs to be more than what it is?" he asked a few minutes later, startling me out of the silent reverie I was in. His face was stoic.

"I thought that what happened back there was more than...you know? I guess I was wrong." I replied. Though I was thinking it, I wasn't about to tell him what I really believed—that all this had been to him was another notch in his tally of girls he had fucked. I cringed, waiting for what was to come.

Instead, I heard him laugh, a loud, genuinely amused laugh. I turned to look at him, unable to speak, unsure what was so funny.

"You kill me," he said between chuckles.

"What are you laughing at?" I asked, getting annoyed.

"You!"

"I didn't realize I was such a funny person."

"Now, now, don't be like that," he said, reaching for my hand. I felt its warmth and couldn't deny how nice it felt in mine, but still, I wanted to pull away.

"Like what? Annoyed that you're making fun of me when I'm trying to have a serious conversation?"

"Yes, precisely like that."

We made another turn and I took note that we were a few minutes from his house.

Good. I couldn't wait to get out of the car.

"Elle, we had sex, that's it. And I appreciate your optimism, but I never said I was looking for more. Just like I'm pretty sure you're not looking for more either. Especially, not right now."

He was right. The entire day had been so dreamlike, I guess I had just assumed that what had happened between us meant he wanted more. And at least he knew I wasn't in the right head space to start a relationship.

"But last night, at the bar, what happened. I like you, I do, but I can't get into a relationship right now. I shouldn't have led you on."

"You didn't lead me on," he said, bewildered. "I don't want you to feel like this needs to be anything more than what it is right now."

We pulled up to Devon's house and he turned off the ignition. We sat in silence, the engine's ticking the only sound between us.

"Look," he began, turning to face me. "I won't deny that I really like you, but the last thing I want is for you to feel that what happened today shouldn't have happened." I felt myself relax a little as he continued. "Today was by far one of the best days I've had in a very, very long time and I hope you enjoyed it as much. But I don't expect you to commit to anything because of it. If you go home and we aren't anything more than these past few hours, that's alright with me."

His honesty amazed me—it was refreshing to have a man actually speak his mind and say how he felt. His hand reached over to mine again, inundating me with relief. He understood what I was going through, probably more than anyone else, and wasn't, as I had feared, taking advantage of it. Much to my own surprise, I was comfortable with the fact that though we'd had sex, it didn't have to go any further than that.

Furthermore, I could see how I had dodged a bullet; it would be so incredibly easy to fall for Devon. Physical attraction aside, I liked him as a person; he was sweet, intelligent and so kind, all of which had been highlighted over the last few days. I became certain that I had done the right thing and that nipping this in the bud had been a good idea.

We got out of the car and I leaned into him, kissing him on the cheek. With a very subtle shift, the corner of his mouth gently grazed mine sending shock waves through me.

"Thank you for today, Devon."

I tried to step back but his hand took mine.

"Why does it have to end now? Come inside for a bit," he suggested, his eyes full of suggestion. "For a drink?"

"But, I thought we just agreed that this wouldn't become more."

"Sure, but that doesn't mean we can't enjoy each other's company a little while longer."

I became weak in the knees just from the look he gave. I knew I should go home to clear my mind—and definitely to take another shower—but I threw caution to the wind. The truth was that I liked being in the bubble of distraction he created. It was nice and warm and incredibly sexy.

"Just for a little while," I said, accepting his offer, as he led me inside.

CHAPTER NINETEEN

I followed Devon through the wood-panelled hallway toward the living room. While he got us drinks, I stood at the windows and watched the lake below. The sun was beginning to lower in the sky, the light getting softer but still making the water glisten and sending sparkles across its surface. I couldn't be sure if it was what had happened between us, or the simple beauty of the day, but I felt a sudden shift within me as if I couldn't possibly dislike Frelighsburg any longer. Its quiet, unassuming beauty was clear to me now and mixed in with my nostalgia for simpler days, I found that I could now understand why so many people fell in love with the area.

Devon walked over with two drinks in hand. It was sweet and orange and entirely too fancy, garnished with a piece of orange peel.

"Wow," I said, taking a sip. "You've outdone yourself."

"I like making things look good." He seemed proud of this fact.

"Just like this house," I added.

"I suppose."

He went to the sofa and I followed. We sat side by side in the large cream-coloured sectional, him putting his feet on the coffee table. He let out a long, relaxed breath and leaned back.

"So," I said, trying to fill the silence. "You're into horses?"

"Love them. Have since I was a kid and my dad used to take me. Never had my own until…" He trailed off, his eyes becoming distant. "Until I got the inheritance."

"Oh, of course," I stuttered. "Well, at least you used it for something that makes you happy." I shook my head, feeling like a fool for what I was saying.

"Hmm," he replied, rubbing his hand up and down his thigh.

"Don't they make you happy, the horses?"

"Yes, they do. But I guess lately I've been looking for something to fill this void. I'm starting to think it might be impossible. I miss my parents so much sometimes and even when I try to escape a little, and try new things, I never feel like that will stop."

He seemed nervous and I felt like I should change the subject. I didn't like the darkness that was seeping out of him.

"I don't think it's ever supposed to stop," I replied, feeling a surge of sadness. "But I guess I should keep that in mind."

"Shit, I didn't mean…I shouldn't have said that," he started, putting his arm around my shoulders. "I'm sorry."

"Don't be. I brought it up."

"True, you did," he winked, playfully.

I laughed with him, feeling at ease yet again. I leaned back against the sofa, feeling his arm around me. I could tell he was watching me.

"Seriously, though, I can't believe I missed it."

"Missed what?"

"You. When we were kids."

"Stop it. You don't know what you're talking about."

"I think I do."

He leaned in and kissed me on my cheek, then my lips. He pulled me by the waist and I turned to him, putting my leg over his lap. He kissed my neck and my collarbone, slowly moving down my chest. I couldn't help but look back at the windows, suddenly feeling shy and exposed.

"Um, can we go to your bedroom?"

"Why?" he asked, his voice muffled, never ceasing his kisses.

"People will see us."

"They won't."

"They might. I saw you, didn't I?"

He sat back up, looking at me with playful annoyance.

"Sure, but I was standing right in front of the window."

He got up and walked over. Not thinking anything of it, I went to stand next to him. Before I knew it, I was in his arms again, but this time he had me pressed against the window.

"Now, they'll definitely see us."

I giggled and let his kisses win me over. Though I surrendered to him, I knew in the back of mind that there was no way I would let him get me naked for the whole world to see, despite what he might be thinking.

He picked me up and carried me to his bedroom. His strength and apparent ease with carrying me up the flight of stairs turned me on even more than I thought possible.

We reached his bedroom, the sight of his bed made me grateful I would now be conscious and remember getting into it. I was giddy with excitement and couldn't believe this was happening again. It was intoxicating, to say the least—the feeling of being drunk off of one another and from wanting each other so bad.

I could get used to this, I thought, my brain now void of doubts and second guesses. We frantically undressed as if we were on a schedule or as if the moment was soon to disappear. The rapidity of it all took second, but once we were sufficiently naked, time slowed down.

I took him in my hand and stroked up and down. He licked his lips as I pushed him back onto the bed. Slowly, I put him in my mouth, pleasantly surprised at how delicious he tasted. A low moan escaped his mouth, making me push him in further. Moving my mouth back and forth, and with gradual pressure, I felt him get harder. I also felt incredibly powerful. He moaned my name and bit his lip, making me continue with even more vigour. I could feel he was getting close to coming as I gently sucked on the tip.

He let out a loud grunt before saying, "Stop."

My eyes bolted open, as I stopped, unsure why. "What's wrong?"

"Nothing is wrong," he said, panting and cradling my face with his hands. "I don't want to come just yet."

I blushed. With one swift move, he flipped me on to my back and then slammed into me hard. Loudly, I screamed, hearing my voice echo in the large room. He held my arms down as he thrust himself into me, his eyes never closing, never breaking their gaze into mine. My legs wrapped around his waist, watching beads of sweat appear on his brow. Our bodies found a rhythm I had never found before, bringing me to my much-needed release. As we came simultaneously, he peered into my eyes, deeper still and I felt something shift within me. Something profound, momentous. I tried to dismiss it and blame it on the orgasm I had just experienced, but I knew deep, deep down it was far more than that.

Gently, he pulled out of me and cradled me in his arms, our foreheads touching. We looked at each other and I couldn't think of one single thing to say. I couldn't even find something funny to break the seriousness of the moment.

He didn't say anything either, making the silence that much more profound. Then, his hand reached up, his fingers brushed the hair out of my face and just rested there. I had never felt anything like it before. His gaze and the way he was holding me—it was a million times more intense than our earlier experiences. But, even acknowledging that I wasn't about to admit it to him.

His words from earlier came back to me. I remembered how he had simplified what was happening between us and had admitted he wasn't trying to turn this into something serious. I had to remind myself of that as much and as often as possible.

"You're so beautiful. You know that?"

"Shut up," I said, the spell now broken. I tried to turn away from him, but he held me tight.

"I won't. Clearly, you haven't been told enough."

"I think you just enjoyed your blow job a little too much."

He laughed his loud, powerful laugh and hugged me against him. "There is no denying that was spectacular, but—"

I cut him off before he could say anything more, putting my finger against his lips. "Shh, don't."

I pressed my lips against his, partly because I wanted him to stop talking, but also because I couldn't resist him. I felt him stiffen against my leg.

"Again? Really?" I giggled, as he turned me over.

CHAPTER TWENTY

The short walk to my parents home felt long as I mulled over the day's events. My legs were still jelly from my day with Devon. It had been difficult to leave his house, not because I didn't want to, but because we found it hard to let go of each other. It was intoxicating being around Devon, but I knew I had to cut it short and return home. I needed to spend some time with my parents and talk things over with them, no matter how hard it might prove to be.

I laughed when I realized how much had happened and how much my world had been turned on its head in such a short time. To think that three days prior my biggest issue was whether or not Paul and I were still an item. It all seemed like ages ago now.

Parked outside my parents' house I noticed a familiar-looking silver Mercedes, making my stomach lurch.

It couldn't be.

I peeked through the driver's side window. As if checking off a list in my mind, I noticed each item one by one. In the cup-holder was the not-nearly-finished cup of coffee. In the centre console was the pack of spearmint gum, the whitening kind. And there, hanging in the back seat as it usually was, was the black pea coat I had bought him for his birthday last year.

This was without a doubt Paul's car.
What the hell was Paul doing here?
Fuming, I went inside. Before I saw anybody, I could hear my mother laughing, loud and boisterously. It was coming from the living room. My father was sitting on the couch, drink in hand, chuckling and my mother sat next to him, laughing hysterically at something Paul had said.

Paul.

He sat across from them, also with a drink in hand. From what I overheard, he was in the middle of telling them about the time I had been so drunk in Cancun, I had slipped and fallen into the pool. The story was usually Paul's go-to when trying to break the ice with people. It always made everyone laugh, excluding me, for obvious reasons.

I managed to clear my throat, announcing my presence.

"Elizabeth," my father said, startled. "Look who just showed up. Why didn't you tell us you were seeing such a funny, young man?"

Paul smiled, inviting me to sit beside him. I refused.

"More importantly," my mother added, "Why didn't you mention Paul at all?"

My cheeks flushed with embarrassment. "Because we're not together anymore," I snapped, eyeing him.

Still in disbelief that Paul was in my parents' living room—let alone in Frelighsburg—I went over to the bar and poured myself a drink. I had never been a fan of hard liquor, but seeing as the only thing on supply was scotch and bourbon, I poured myself a glass of the expensive single malt and chugged it down in one gulp. I noticed my father's disapproving look, but he said nothing.

"What are you doing here, Paul?" I asked, the Scotch warming me up. I blinked as my eyes watered, a little from the drink, a little from anger.

"I figured I would come and visit," he began. "I felt horrible knowing you were going through all this by yourself."

He grinned at my parents as if looking for approval for his good deed. They nodded in agreement and I hoped they weren't stupid enough to fall for his obvious pandering.

"But how did you know where I was?" I had never even told Paul where my parents lived, so to see him here now made it all the more confusing.

"You didn't tell him where you were going?" my mother asked, a look of shocked disbelief on her face matching her equally appalled tone. I rolled my eyes at her and shook my head as if trying to tell her to shut up. We could deal with my white lies later.

"I spoke to Mrs. Benson," Paul explained.

I didn't have to hear the rest to know where he was headed. Little, sociable Mrs. Benson would chat with anyone let alone gorgeous, charming Paul. Of course, I had never imagined he would care enough to investigate my whereabouts. If I had, I definitely would have asked her to keep it to herself.

"After that, it wasn't hard Googling *Williams Orchard*," he tacked on, proud of himself. "Did you know your family's the only Williams family in Phillipsburg?"

"Frelighsburg," we all corrected simultaneously.

"Right," he walked over to me, taking me in his arms.

I stood, unable to move, stunned. I still couldn't come to grips with the fact that he had come all this way, had put in the actual effort to find me and was at the same time putting me in a very uncomfortable position. I also couldn't help but compare his embrace to that of Devon's. Whereas I felt safe and comforted in Devon's strong arms, in Paul's I felt restricted and especially cold. Stuck in his hold, unsure what to do next, I felt the enormity of his presence deep in the pit of my stomach.

"So, where have you been all day?" he asked, loosening his grip.

All day?

I wondered exactly when he had arrived. I struggled to think of something to say. It wasn't like I had taken the time to think of an alibi, I never dreamt I would need one, either.

"I went horseback riding," I said, giving him as much of the truth as I could, without revealing too much.

"Horseback riding?" my father asked, cynical. A look crossed his face, but before I knew what it could mean, it was gone.

"Your daughter never ceases to amaze me," Paul said, beaming with pride. "She's always up for new things."

I then caught sight of the Paul I knew so well. His cold, arrogant eyes stared at me, his tone accusing. I grabbed Paul by the hand and led him outside.

As we reached the front yard, I began to pace.

"You don't seem too happy to see me." He stood his arms crossed but smirking.

I glared at him, my pulse racing. "Are you kidding me? Why would I be happy to see you, Paul?" I noticed him recoil and knew that I was yelling a little too loudly. "Did you ever stop to think that maybe I didn't want you here? And besides, we broke up! What does it matter where I am and what I'm doing?"

"We didn't really break up now did we?" he answered tilting his head to the side almost defiantly. "We made up, remember?"

Memories of our evening together came rushing back and I began to laugh. It felt good to let it out, to acknowledge the absurdity of it all.

"You think that because we had sex that means we're back together?" I approached him. "Did you fail to notice that I was incredibly vulnerable that night? You took advantage of me. That was not a reconciliation."

He was shaking his head from side to side, as if in complete disagreement with what I was saying. It reminded me of when we had first met.

I had been interviewing at his company, a complete ball of nerves when he had barged in on the meeting. My potential boss told him he was interrupting, but Paul didn't seem bothered—he was the CFO after all. He stood, shaking his head—just as he was doing now—and eyed me. I had felt completely intimidated at first, even shrinking back into my chair a little. But after a moment, I came to the realization that he wasn't looking at me with contempt, but rather with attraction. The intimidation vanished. Later on, once the interview had ended, he had found me in the elevator and asked me out.

That was over two years ago. Back then, I used to find his arrogance somewhat appealing and I had misinterpreted it as confidence. Now, the look that had once made me attracted to him was instead making my blood boil.

Facing him, quite literally standing up to his tall figure—as much as my short stature could allow—I let the words spill out.

"I can't keep up this shit anymore!" I snapped. "I am not here for your pleasure, for you to just throw to the curb once you've got your fill," I took a deep breath. "Too much has happened over the weekend and—,"

"I know, Liz, I know." He said, interrupting me. He took me into his arms, catching me completely by surprise. "I understand how close I came to losing you for good and it freaked me out."

I felt him breathe in. My cheek pressed against his chest, I could hear his heart thumping. This was the first time Paul had ever shown so much emotion and it shook me. It seemed honest, but it was so unlike him, I couldn't be sure it was at all genuine.

"You're the one who ended things."

"I know and that was stupid of me."

He pulled away a little, his eyes meeting mine. The sincerity in them, if that's what it was, reached into my gut and tugged at something. Maybe it was our history together, maybe it was just the culmination of the entire weekend's unrest, but I found something strangely comforting in his presence.

"I don't know, Paul," I said, my words laced with legitimate uncertainty.

I saw visions of Devon, felt his weight on me, his lips on mine.

Should I tell Paul?

It would inevitably break his heart. Then again, wasn't I

finished with Paul; hadn't that ship sailed, to say the least? Why was I yet again even remotely considering taking him back?

"Liz, please give me a second chance," he begged. "At least let me come with you tomorrow."

"Tomorrow?" I looked up at him, confused.

"The funeral."

Of course, the funeral. With all the distractions I'd had, namely because of Devon, I had completely let it slip my mind.

Paul hugged me again and this time I didn't feel the immediate need to push him away. The entire town would be at the funeral and so would Devon. What difference would it make if Paul was there too? It would prove to be a tough day, regardless of whose company I was in. Plus, I still didn't know what to do about the orchards and that was a much more pressing issue than whether or not Paul stuck around.

My mind raced a mile a minute. Paul leaned in for a kiss and I thought of Devon again, imagining him watching us. I felt guilty. I should have told him about Paul. Then again, I had truly believed Paul was history. There wasn't anything to tell Devon about.

I felt my temples pounding, the stress bringing on the worst headache. Paul's lips brushed against mine, desperately wanting a kiss but not forcing it. I hesitated, not knowing what to do and hating myself for it. His sudden show of affection had stirred everything, setting my world even more on its edge. I didn't know what I wanted anymore, didn't know why the universe was sending me so many curve balls. I felt entirely lost.

"Are you coming in to help with dinner or staying out here all night?" my mother shouted from the house.

Paul pulled away, looking disappointed, but I felt a rush of relief flood over me.

"Let's go in," I said.

CHAPTER TWENTY-ONE

Paul was uncharacteristically cooperative as my parents cooked dinner. Being my usual unhelpful self, I sat at the kitchen island, watching them. Paul cut some vegetables and made a salad, all while chatting, and charming as much as he could.

I couldn't recognize this person that stood before me. In all our years together, he had never cooked me anything, had never been so delightful. If I didn't suspect his motives, he would have won me over.

I thought back to what he had said outside and wondered if he was being honest with me—was he really worried he'd lost me?

It was true that I was glad he was being so nice, but I was also aware that this was probably just a way to lure me back in. We could easily get back together, but once we were back in Montreal, in our regular day-to-day, he would without a doubt go back to the way he always was—arrogant and dismissive. I was sure we would end up broken up, yet again, within a matter of weeks, that's assuming we even made it that far.

Since I had returned home, and obviously since being with Devon, I couldn't for the life of me understand why I had invested so much time with Paul. Maybe my self-esteem was to blame. Maybe I didn't think too highly of myself.

But as we all sat for dinner, Paul squeezing himself next to me, I realized that I deserved better. And thanks to Devon, I now knew I could get better.

Paul's arm rubbed against mine and made me feel stifled, but I held back from pushing him away. Instead, I went after some answers to questions that had been bothering me.

"Why didn't you tell me the Barretts had died?" I asked blatantly, as my mother passed the mashed potatoes.

"Why does that matter?" she replied, her hands dropping to the table. "You didn't even know them."

"They were our neighbours. Why didn't you mention it at some point?"

"It's not like you would have been interested. Would you?" she hissed, her eyes piercing straight through me.

"What's that supposed to mean?" I knew exactly where this was headed.

"You know," she waved a hand in the air, flippantly. "What with being busy with other things."

"Other things. Right," I pursed my lips. "Don't tell me you're still mad I didn't come home last Christmas."

"To be fair, Alex, Corinne," Paul interrupted. "That was entirely my fault. I got a great deal on these tickets to Cancun and I wanted to spoil her."

He reached over and wrapped his arm around me, squeezing. I glared at him, wishing that looks could kill.

"That's incredibly thoughtful of you, Paul," my mother said, beaming.

"Hang on a minute," I snapped. "Why am I the bad guy for missing Christmas, but he's a darling for taking me on the trip?"

"Elizabeth, let's not fight," my dad said.

"I'm not trying to start a fight, Dad," I replied, looking at him. "I'm just looking for answers, but as always, I get the double standard in this house."

"You're father's right. Let's not fight," my mom said calmly, dismissing me.

Her eyes looked down but it seemed to me that she had a small grin on her face. I knew she was thankful for my father's interruption and was just hoping I would let it drop. But I wasn't about to.

"You're right," I said, still angered. "It doesn't matter what I do. No matter what, I've always been the one who's in the wrong." They looked at me with uncertainty in their eyes. "And let's face it, Mom. You've never stopped being mad at me since…" I stopped myself, thinking maybe I was going too far.

"Go on, say it," Corinne challenged, trying to call my bluff.

"Since what?" my father asked, casting inquisitive glances at my mother and me.

I shook my head and closed my eyes. I knew I shouldn't answer him and that I should let it lie, but I had brought it up and the urge to get it off my chest was greater than me.

"Since Mom's affair," I said.

I could feel the air get sucked out of the room. Paul shifted in his seat, clearly uncomfortable.

Good for him.

My father leaned back in his chair and crossed his arms. "Let's not talk about that tonight. We have a guest and—,"

"Elizabeth, I've paid for my mistakes," my mother interrupted, defensively. "And in many ways—ways you don't even know about—I am still paying."

She hung her head defeated. Pieces started falling into place as if an unsolved puzzle had finally been completed. In that instant, I knew, deep down inside, what she meant.

"Grandma? That's why she didn't give you the business?"

It now made perfect sense. My grandmother was fully aware of the affair but had told me to stay out of it. She knew that I resented the fact that my father had stayed and that it had all been swept under the rug. I had always assumed Dolores had done the same, but now I could see that clearly, she hadn't.

"Why didn't you tell me?"

"Tell you what? That because of a mistake I made years

ago, your grandmother would do something like this?" My mother's eyes began to swell up with tears. "How do you admit such a shameful thing to your daughter?"

Her question lingered in the uncomfortable silence.

I didn't know what to say. I couldn't believe my grandmother would do something so spiteful. It was true that my mother and she had never been very close. But still, to go so far as to withhold something this important and which was rightfully theirs or at the very least my father's? Why was he being punished for my mother's actions? I suddenly felt very cold.

My father reached over and took my mother's hand. The fact that he could still love her, still show affection toward her after what she had done never ceased to amaze me. I looked at Paul who seemed incredibly confused and uneasy and I knew that no matter what, I could never love him the same way my parents loved each other. Suddenly, it all became clear to me. We definitely didn't belong together. I didn't even want to stick around and pretend any longer.

"I'm sorry to have brought all this up," I said, getting up. "I'm going to go lie down. I'm not feeling too well."

"Paul," my father said, clearing his throat. "You're welcomed to sleep in the guest room tonight."

I waited to hear Paul's answer, curious if he would be bold enough to accept when him and I both knew he should drive home instead.

"Sure, that would be great," he said, winking at me. "Thanks, Alex."

I winced and walked away, amazed at how quickly Paul had become so at ease with my parents and repulsed by his obvious desire to torment me a little while longer.

In the quiet solitude of my bedroom, I sank onto the bed and stared at the ceiling. I could hear my parents and Paul talking downstairs, their muffled voices and laughter telling me the mood had lightened considerably.

For me, unfortunately, it wasn't the case. I was still irate with Paul for showing up unannounced—a fact, I now realized, he had never apologized for—and I was also completely stunned by my grandmother's actions.

I understood her mistrust of my mother, but to keep the business from my father as some sort of twisted punishment for what my mother had done? That seemed so unlike Dolores. And then to top it off, she had given me the business, almost as if she was rubbing it in my parents' faces. Shoving my head into the pillow, I screamed out my frustration.

I could still hear them downstairs, moving their conversation from the dining room to the den. I needed someone to talk to and the only person I could think of was only a few hundred feet from me but in an entirely different house. All I wanted to do was to see Devon and explain it all—why I left town, why I didn't want to come back. I needed to tell him about Paul and how I felt about our messed up relationship. More importantly, I needed to be clear and tell Devon how I felt about him.

I looked out my window hoping for a glimpse of his house, hoping to see what he was doing, but the view was just shy. It was past ten o'clock, so I assumed he'd be home, but I had no idea. The more I thought about him the less I was able to sit still and the more I wanted his touch, desperate to have his arms around me. I began pacing the room, impatient.

I had to see him.

After a while, I heard my mother go to bed. Opening my door just slightly, I listened and heard my dad and Paul chatting downstairs. Paul was droning on about some wild Peruvian adventure he had taken in his twenties. It was a boring and over-rated story that I had heard far too many times, but to my benefit, I knew it was a long one. They would be busy for a while, giving me the perfect window to escape through.

As quietly as I could, I tiptoed past my parents' bedroom, went downstairs, past the living room and went out through the back veranda.

CHAPTER TWENTY-TWO

I reached Devon's door and paused. Much to my dismay, the resolve I had felt had all but vanished during the walk over. I could see a light on through his windows and hoped he was still awake. I tried to imagine how things would go. In my mind, I would speak my peace and after everything had gone according to plan, he would take me in his arms and lead me inside. I could almost feel the warmth of him, of his arms wrapped around me, of his deft fingers making their way across my skin.

With a shiver of excitement combined with some serious trepidation, I knocked meekly. The seconds ticked by like hours. There was no answer. I thought that maybe he hadn't heard me when, finally, after what seemed like an eternity, he opened the door. He was shirtless, his jeans hanging off his hips. He had paint on his fingers and hands, plus a little smudge on his cheek.

"Hey," he said, his face neutral.

"Hi, can I come in?" I asked, sheepishly. There was a quick glimpse of something, maybe annoyance, but I couldn't be sure. "Unless I'm interrupting?"

I tried to peek inside, but he kept the door only slightly ajar, blocking my view. He paused, and, after what I took as some genuine consideration on his part, he stepped aside, without saying a word. I followed behind him as he made his way down the hall, the whole time getting a distinct impression that I wasn't quite welcome.

We stepped through two sliding doors into a room I hadn't even noticed earlier in the day. Canvases were strewn all over the room, varying in sizes. There were landscapes, both local and exotic. I saw this was an art studio—*his* art studio—and I felt as if I was being let in on a huge secret.

Each painting, vivid and captivating, amazed me. He had a definite talent. Passing a large wooden work table, which was covered in paints, brushes, and rags, I touched the worn, old wood. Beside it sat a large canvas on an easel. Though it appeared to be a portrait, it was still incomplete. He was standing in front of it, his back slightly turned to me.

"I didn't know you were an artist," I said, approaching the unfinished work. Was there anything this man couldn't do?

"I paint as a hobby. Artists get paid for their work."

"Sure, but usually not until they're dead," I joked, hoping to lighten his dark mood, but his face remained indifferent. Clearly, he was upset, but I had no idea why. I chose to ignore it and continued talking. "You've got an amazing eye, Devon," I looked closer at the canvas, appreciating each brush stroke. "Who's the subject?" My assumption went straight to Nicole, though the hair colour didn't seem to match her shade.

"No one," he said, brusquely. I felt a coldness in his words, in his body that brought a chill to my bones. Something was definitely off. "Why are you here, Ellie?"

It bothered me that he hadn't called me Elle. Strangely, I found that I had become used to the nickname and not hearing him use it stung a little.

"I wanted to talk to you, but clearly it's a bad time."

I waited.

"Actually, it is a bad time. I'm not in the best of moods." His tone was curt as he returned to his painting, his back to me again.

"And are you going to tell me why or just keep up this

bullshit?" I crossed my arms. "If you want me to leave, just say so."

He let out a long sigh.

"Yeah, maybe you should go back. You wouldn't want to keep your boyfriend waiting." My heart sank into my stomach as he turned to look at me, his eyes filled with anger and hurt. "I saw you kissing him."

So I had been right. He had seen Paul and me together. I thought back to earlier and how I had wanted to push Paul away. *Why hadn't I?*

"That's Paul, and he's not my boyfriend," I let out a nervous giggle, immediately regretting it.

"I don't find this funny." He went back to painting. "Why did you tell me you weren't seeing anyone?"

"Because I'm not. Not really," I was exasperated, letting out a breath filled with frustration. "We're not together, not anymore. There was nothing to tell you about."

"It sure didn't look like that to me."

"Look, Devon, I'm sorry for what you saw," I said, feeling the inadequacy of the words. "I had no idea he would show up. I didn't even tell him I was here. I'm sure it surprised me just as much as it did you."

"Don't presume to know how this makes me feel."

His brush was assaulting the canvas now, paint streaking across its surface. I could see his neck turning red with anger. I couldn't believe this was happening.

"You're right," I replied, guilt-stricken. "Again, you have no idea how sorry I am—"

"I heard you the first time. Stop apologizing. There's nothing to apologize for."

"But there is," I got closer to him, stopping just shy of touching him. "I need you to believe me. There is nothing between Paul and I and there hasn't been for a very long time."

"I might find it easier to believe you if you had just told me about him in the first place," he said, facing me now. I nodded, filled with shame. He was right, absolutely so, and I couldn't even bear to look him in the eye. "And, if there really is nothing between the two of you, then what the hell is he still doing here?"

"I've been asking myself the same thing. Unfortunately, I can't just send him home," I said, knowing very well that I could have. "He's kind of an immovable force." Devon kept painting, his intensity not diminished in the least. I watched him work, mesmerized and suspended, waiting for him to speak. When he didn't, I continued. "You need to understand that I never thought he'd show up here."

He snickered.

"So you were hoping to keep him a secret then? Tell me," he continued, putting down his brush, challenging me. "Are you upset that he showed up or that I caught you with him?"

"Both?" I attempted honesty, hoping it would fix this. He was right, I should have told him. I felt horrible for my dishonesty. "I hate that he's here, but I also didn't see the point of telling you about him because we're over. Totally. Fucking. Over."

"You might believe that," he said, picking up his brush again, "But it doesn't change the fact that he's in your house right now."

A feeling of supreme guilt came over me; I couldn't stand knowing I had been the cause of his pain. Here I was, chastising my mother for her infidelities when I had two men on the outskirts. I had assumed Devon was a man who was tough as nails, but instead I had clearly affected him. And despite his constant reassurances throughout the day that this was nothing serious, I could tell now, by his obvious fragility, that he'd been lying.

His wounded expression coaxed something out of me—a protectiveness of sorts. I wrapped my arms around his chest, resting my cheek on his back. I felt him still, making my heart flutter, but was relieved when he didn't pull away.

"He might be over there, but I'm not," I whispered.

His chest rose and fell with a rapid breath, as he threw his brush down. He turned to face me, my arms not letting go. Following a brief moment of hesitation, a million things running through his eyes, he ran his thumb across my lips. I could feel the wetness of the paint but didn't care. Immediately, all my worries seemed to melt away. All thoughts of Paul and our drawn-out, tedious relationship vanished.

Urgently, I pulled Devon tightly against me. His lips aggressively parted mine, as my fingers wound themselves into his hair. Slowly, he led me backward. I felt something behind me—the table. Grabbing my hips, he turned me around, bending me over. I could feel his erection against me and in one swift move, he lowered my pants. The combination of being pinned against the table's hard surface and the emotions coursing through me made it hard for me to catch my breath.

I felt his hand brush gently against my bottom. He hovered, just above the skin's surface, making soft circles. I gyrated with every move he made, moaning in sync, my heart racing with anticipation. His hands were strong and firm against my bottom and I could feel the roughness of his hard-worked fingers. With a strong and sudden smack, he spanked me. Despite the twinge of pain that shot through me and the surprise of it, I found myself enjoying it. I didn't know if it was just kink or rather some kind of punishment for pissing him off, but either way, I felt like I needed it—wanted it.

After a few moments, when the sting died down, he spanked me a second time, making me cry out. Still, I wanted more.

He leaned over me and whispered in my ear, "You have no idea how long I've wanted to do that to you."

And with a swift, forceful thrust, he was in me, pushing my thighs into the table's edge. The pain of it was almost too much for me to take. Almost.

With one hand, he grabbed a fistful of my hair and held my shoulder with the other. He began to drive himself further and further, harder and harder. I couldn't control it; I screamed out his name, smacking the table in sheer ecstasy. My nails dug into the wooden surface. I could hear my ass slamming against his hips, the sound propelling my arousal through the roof. Moaning louder than I had ever moaned before—or with anyone for that matter—I pushed into him as hard as I could. I immediately felt myself tighten and convulse, coming undone, groaning a guttural groan that came from somewhere deep inside me.

Exhausted after finding our release, he rested on top of me, kissing my neck. Though I was out of breath, my legs still shaking from my orgasm, I didn't want to move. Lying satiated, I tried in vain to remember the last time I had enjoyed sex so much. It had always been something to fill a void, literally and figuratively. But these encounters with Devon had brought on a different feeling—a feeling of pure joy and contentment. I had been able to let go completely and to lose myself in the moment, which was filling me with awe and trepidation.

It was scary not being able to resist Devon; the way he could make me forget everything and could take me in with his body. I had never felt so under someone else's control. No other man had ever awoken such feelings.

"Want to get washed up?" he suggested, stripping naked.

I leaned against the table, watching him. He was truly a sight to behold and yet again showed no signs of shyness, standing naked in front of me. He reached for me, pulled me closer and started removing my clothes. I felt shy but I didn't feel the need to hide. He smiled and led me to the bathroom.

CHAPTER TWENTY-THREE

He stepped into the tub first, offering his hand to help me in. I sat down slowly, letting my body adjust to the heat of the water. My skin was sensitive, especially in the places where he had spanked me, but as I rested my head against his chest, I felt at ease and let out a long sigh.

"This is all so messed up," I admitted while he massaged my shoulders. "I don't know what I'm going to do."

"About which part exactly?" he whispered, skimming my earlobe with his lips. "Your ex or the other stuff?"

"The other stuff. The ex is the easiest part," I shook my head. "How can I possibly make the right decision? I'm leaving after…the funeral."

I let the word hang in the air, hearing its echoes in the room. It had been lingering there all the while but at that moment I was struck with the finality of it. I had not even taken the time to prepare, mentally or emotionally, for laying my grandmother to rest.

I had always hated funerals in general. I hated the feeling of death, of eternally resting in the cold, dark soil. I wished my grandmother had chosen cremation rather than being buried, not that it would have bothered me any less. Still, respecting her wishes and seeing her casket lowered into the ground were two entirely different things.

My breathing became shallow as panic struck me. I could feel myself tense, my eyes blur. I tried to take slow, deep breaths.

"Relax," Devon said, stroking his hands up and down my arms. "It's going to be alright."

"Is it?" I asked, doubt seeping into my words. If anyone knew about the sadness I was feeling it was him. He had lost both parents in one night. Compared to that, the death of my grandmother after a long, well-lived life wasn't really the same. "How did you do it?"

"With my parents?" His voice was low.

"Sorry, never mind, you don't need to answer that," I regretted bringing it up.

"No, it's fine," he said, kissing my head. "It's hard, Elle, no doubt about that. Actually, I don't think the word *hard* does it justice. It's like everything you thought was good and right suddenly feels wrong, upside-down. And then once you come to grips with their death—which you don't ever, really—then you have to put them in a box and never see their face again. It's the worst thing I've ever had to do."

I swallowed hard, the depth of his sorrow hitting me.

"You seem to have dealt with it reasonably well."

"I had to, for Valerie," he said, kissing my shoulder. "Sometimes, it's what life gives you and you have to find a way to get through it. If not for yourself, then for the others around you—the ones who need and love you."

I thought of my parents and realized I hadn't spoken to them about all of this. I had been so wrapped in my own world I hadn't even taken the time to see what they thought or how they felt. I had let my anger against my mother take over and was now starting to see how this entire situation was affecting them. I had been so selfish—I should have talked to them.

"My parents. My dad..."

"They'll be fine, Elle," Devon reassured me as if reading my thoughts, "With whatever you decide to do."

"How can you know that for sure?"

"Because whatever you decide, so long as you're doing it for the right reasons and so long as it makes you happy, then they'll have to accept that."

His logic was simplistic, to say the least, and I highly doubted it would be that easy, but he did have a point. I needed to figure out what I would do with the business and soon. Tomorrow would be filled with inquisitive people, all wanting to know the future of the Williams' Family Orchards.

"Shit," I said, sitting straight up. "I'm going to have to say something, aren't I? At the service. I didn't even think about that."

"Not if you don't want to," Devon said, nonchalantly. "I am sure people will understand if you don't. They know it's harder on you."

"You can't say that. It has no right to be harder on me."

The nagging voice in my head was back, reminding me of all the reasons why I had failed my grandmother, why I should be ashamed of the granddaughter I had become. Surely, I owed her more. The guilt was permeating my each and every thought. It flooded me with all the possible choices I would have to face. No matter what I did to distract myself from them, it was foolish to think they would disappear. Devon shifted a little bringing me back to the moment. Wrapped comfortably in his embrace, another issue popped up in my brain.

"What are we doing here, Devon?"

"Taking a bath isn't that obvious?" he said, laughing. His hand rubbed my stomach and started wandering a little lower.

"Be serious," I snapped, stopping his hand. "This can't work."

He sighed. "Nothing is happening, Elle. We're just having fun."

"That's not all that's going on here and you know it. Don't pretend with me." I felt him breathe in. "I'm officially your boss now. I don't live here and I'm definitely not moving back."

"Why do you hate it here so much?"

"I don't hate it, but my life's in the city," I answered as vaguely as I could. I knew the answer to his question was far too complex to delve into at that moment.

"Alright," he replied doubtfully. "So we don't live in the same town, that's not exactly a huge issue. Montreal isn't that far."

"It isn't, but it's far enough for me. I don't do long distance."

"I wouldn't say an hour's drive is long distance."

"Fine," I was getting annoyed that he was being so persistent. "Jokes aside," I added, fearing he would be sarcastic again, "Could you handle taking orders from me?"

"So, is that your decision, then?" he asked, changing the subject. "You're keeping the Orchards?"

I shook my head. "I don't have much of a choice, do I? She wanted me to take care of it. I have to."

He paused. "Right. Then that's that. This will end here. No big deal."

His assertive response shut me down and, unsure what else I could say, I leaned back against his chest. Though he was acting like this was merely some weekend fling, nothing serious, I knew there was more between us than he was letting on. Something profound had been ignited between the two of us and there was definitely no turning back. I knew as well as he did that business or not, what we had started was intense, passionate and there was no running or hiding from it.

"Devon, be honest, if I were your boss, could we really just be friends?"

"Elle..."

"Please, answer me."

He reached his hand down lower and the feeling sent shivers all over my warm body.

"Just friends? Probably, not. No."

I turned to face him, seeing his playful grin. He raised his hand to my cheek, and I kissed his fingers. I couldn't deny the feelings that were growing inside of me and from my side anyhow, I knew they would soon develop into something much, much more than physical. Hell, if I was being brutally honest with myself, they already had.

His emerald eyes looked deep into mine, searching, longing. Remembering how I had hurt him earlier, the memory broke my heart and I knew that if I let things continue I would probably have to hurt him all over again one day. And we both didn't deserve that.

I kissed him as passionately as I could and stepped out of the bath.

"Where do you think you're going?" he said, holding my hand tightly.

"I have to go."

"Elle, I was kidding. If you want us to be friends, co-workers, whatever, I'll do it. You can stay here tonight. I'll even give you my bed."

"I don't think I'll get much sleep as it is, but I need to be alone." Right now, he was a distraction—though an incredibly gorgeous and pleasant one—and I needed clarity. "I'm sorry for coming over. I only wanted to clear the air."

"Hey, come on, don't go," he pleaded.

There wasn't an ounce of me that didn't want to step back into the warm water and lie with him. I fought off the desire and shook my head. I knew I had to leave.

"I'm sorry, but I have to," I said, wrapping myself in a towel.

Picking up my clothes from the studio's floor, I got dressed quickly, expecting him to come in and stop me. When he didn't, I left with a pang of disappointment in my chest.

It was for the best, I reminded myself.

CHAPTER TWENTY-FOUR

The house seemed quiet as I walked up to it, but still, I didn't take a chance and went in from the back. I was opening the patio door when I heard someone clear their throat.

"Dad? What are you doing up so late?" He was barely visible in the darkness.

"I could ask the same of you," he replied. "I couldn't sleep."

I took the seat next to him, wrapping myself in the blanket I found on the chair. A cold front had definitely crept in during the last few hours, turning the warm weather of late into a chilly evening.

"I had to get out of there," I said, not knowing what else I could say without telling him too much. I figured he didn't really need to know more. "Dinner was a little too much for me."

"Ellie, you know I understand how you feel, but you're not going to hold a grudge against your mother forever, are you?"

I sighed. I was much too tired to hash up this topic once again with my dad. "I don't know. Hopefully not."

"She feels awful for what she did. You must know that."

"I'm sure she feels awful, Dad. Who wouldn't feel shitty

after getting caught cheating? I'm not sure I can forgive her. Not like you did."

"It took time for me to find the capacity to forgive her. It wasn't easy or something I took lightly."

"Are you sure? Because it didn't seem that way. You just turned the other cheek and let her come home like it was nothing. Like she'd *done* nothing."

"That's not exactly how it happened. But you were too young anyhow. There's a lot you were protected from."

I shook my head, wishing I'd gone straight to bed. "Why does everyone feel the need to protect me from everything? I feel like everyone keeps lying to me."

"Alright, that's fair. Then, what would you have done, if you'd been in my shoes."

"I would have been mad, infuriated. I would have told her to fuck off. I would have said that if we weren't good enough for her, she didn't deserve to come back home."

"If *we* weren't good enough? Is that how you feel? That she cheated on both of us?"

"In a way, yes," I replied, barely more than a whisper.

He nodded, slowly, stroking his chin as he did when he was deep in thought.

I needed to put an end to this before it went any further than it had to, or worse, before my dams crumbled and my brave exterior vanished. "But you know what? It doesn't matter how I feel about it. What matters is whether or not you're happy. And if you are, then who am I to judge?"

I assumed that was it for our conversation. Knowing my father and his usual reserve when talking about his feelings, I didn't see the need to press on. Yet, I couldn't hide my surprise when he turned to me and spoke.

"Ellie, do you know what your grandmother told me when she found out about the affair? She told me about a man named Robert. She used to call him Bob."

My breath caught and I knew what he was about to say—my assumption had been right.

"She told me how they had been friends, very good friends,

for years. She'd known him nearly as long as she'd known your grandfather." His eyes shot across the lake, something like anger flashing through them. He continued. "She admitted to me that there had been more between them than friendship, not for long, but for a little while when I was a kid. Anyway, she admitted she'd been unfaithful and it broke my heart. I'd never known, never had any doubt in my mind that she and my dad were nothing but incredibly happy together."

My mind was racing, trying to wrap itself around the idea of my grandmother being unfaithful. I suddenly felt like the ground my perception of her was built on had shifted and crumbled. I had supposed there was a chance she'd dated Bob, but that was after my grandfather had died, not while he was alive. I couldn't grasp how she could have done it and how Bob had been her lover.

"You must have hated her," I replied, imagining my father's anger when hearing this heart-breaking revelation.

He took a breath and leaned closer, as if what he was about to say was crucial, then he smiled. "Maybe a little at first, but it faded. She made me understand why she had done it."

I looked at him, unsure how someone could validate such a betrayal of another's trust.

"The way she saw it, she wasn't happy in her relationship. There was a void and though she didn't know what it was at the time, she knew something important was missing. She had to go out and find it."

I tilted my head, skeptically. "She didn't have to go out and find it. That's what people say so they don't feel as guilty for what they've done. There's always a way out."

"Maybe. It's easy to think that now," he conceded. "But you have to remember, at the time she told me this, I was in the same situation she had been. At the time, I could understand what she meant. It was partly my fault." I rolled my eyes, which he saw and acknowledged. "I know it's hard to believe but in a marriage, sometimes you drift from one another and you don't even see it happening. Your grandmother was right—it was my fault. I didn't admit that to her then, of course. The more I thought about it, and once I let my anger dissipate, I could see how your mother wasn't happy at home. I was guilty of making her promises when we first met, even when we got married, that I never kept. Sadly, had I been more observant at the time, then maybe I would have seen it before it happened."

I watched him deep in thought as if he was letting his words sink in once more. Maybe he was hoping that had he done things differently back then, maybe the outcome would have been different.

Then, I remembered how he had seemed to have forgiven her rather quickly and how that had never sat well with me. It didn't make sense that such a kind person like my father could get hurt like that, and get over it so effortlessly.

"Still," I said, my voice cracking a little. "Even if you could accept that it was somewhat your fault, you didn't need to forgive her. You didn't need to stay with her."

He smiled and looked down at his hands. He started playing with his wedding ring, turning it in circles around his finger.

"It's a shame that you've never been in love."

"I've been in love," I replied defensively, a little insulted by the assumption. "I've been with Paul for years."

"That's not love," he said. "I'm not sure what that is, but it's definitely not what I mean when I say *love*. You're not happy with the guy and I don't blame you. He's not right for you."

"Be it as it may, there have been others before him." He looked at me as if he wasn't buying what I was selling. "There have been!"

"If that were the case, honey, then you wouldn't be sitting here, asking me why I forgave your mother and why I needed to stay with her. You'd know."

Inside the house, a light inside was turned on and we both knew it would be my mother, coming down to check on him.

"That's my cue," he said, standing up.

He kissed me on the forehead, gently, lovingly. He lingered

if only for a second. After a moment, he wished me a good night and went in.

I put my legs up on his chair, wrapping the blanket tightly around me. I felt the weight of my father's words drop down on my shoulders. In the past few days, I had discovered Dolores had been an entirely different woman than I had known. She wasn't deeply honest, loyal or even generous—at least not without conditions. I felt like she had betrayed me, as had everyone who had known about her secrets but hadn't cared enough to share. I wondered if Devon knew about all of this. Surely he hadn't or else why would he have had such respect for her?

Then again, what did I know?

Maybe he was fully aware of all this and instead chose to ignore it. He did live in this town where secrets didn't stay secret for very long—it was almost inevitable to have heard rumours or been privy to the gossip.

Devon.

My brain returned to earlier, in his home, the feeling of excitement, of pleasure and comfort I had felt. How I had not wanted to leave. A cold gust of wind suddenly kicked up, amplifying the goosebumps I already had. Was my dad right—had I never really been in love before? I had always thought I had been. I had said the words more than once and not just to Paul. I had always believed I was happy and content in my past relationships. There had never been any doubt, at least not in my mind, that there had been love present. At least, there had been no doubt until now.

My father's attachment and devotion to my mother, something I had always seen as weakness, was strong and there was no doubt in his mind that he was meant to be with her. Was that it? Was that the way to know for sure if you were in love? That you would go through anything, forgive anything, to be with them?

I was growing more and more tired, but I knew I wouldn't get much sleep as long as these thoughts kept running around in my head. Still, I went inside with hopes that maybe I could at least quiet this unexpected heaviness I now had lingering in my heart.

Sunday, April 23rd

CHAPTER TWENTY-FIVE

I wasn't sure I had gotten much sleep if any at all, but my day started with me feeling more confused and uncertain than I had the previous night. Now, everything felt new and messy. After a quick shower, I put on my black dress and a cardigan. The sun was bright and shining, announcing yet another beautiful spring day.

My father was making breakfast in the kitchen. My mother, on the other hand, was in the bathroom getting ready. With no sign of Paul, I took the opportunity to pick up where we had left off the night before.

"Good morning," I said, pouring some coffee. "How did you sleep?"

"Morning, sweetie," he said, putting some whisked eggs into a pan. "Not too bad considering. How about you?"

"I've had better nights." I sat down at the kitchen island and watched my dad cut some fruit. "I can do that if you want."

"Thanks, but I need to keep my hands and head busy." He lowered his head, his eyes glassy, and I immediately wished I had taken the time to speak to him earlier.

"Dad, I know I haven't said it before, but I'm really sorry about Grandma." I reached across the island and placed my hand on his.

"I'm sorry, too," he said, smiling but I could tell it was a front.

He was sticking to his macho guns and refusing to let his emotions show. I couldn't blame him.

"What am I going to do?" I asked.

He didn't need more explanation. He knew very well what I meant.

"You'll do what you can and make her proud. That's what you've always done."

"Why does everyone make it sound so simple?"

"Who's everyone?" his eyes perked up.

I clammed up, trying desperately to find a way out.

"Is that where you went off to last night?" he said, scrambling the eggs and letting them simmer. I looked away, pretending I hadn't heard his question. "Fine, fine, don't tell me. But I will say you seemed pretty happy when you came back. I've never seen you look that happy." He turned the burner off and brought the eggs to our plates. He added some bacon and fruit and handed me my breakfast. "Bon appétit, ma belle."

I dug into the food, happy to have something to fill my mouth and help me avoid his questions.

My mother walked in, dressed in a black pantsuit and cream-coloured shirt, her eyes puffy but her makeup impeccable. "Good morning."

Kissing her on the cheek, my father held her against him for a moment. It was a rare sight, I felt, but I saw something between them that I had not seen in what seemed like ages.

"Sleep well?" my mother asked, sitting next to me, as my father prepared a plate for her.

"OK, I guess," I lied. "You?"

"Not a wink. Today's going to be hard for all of us."

Her words couldn't have been truer. We ate in silence and I thought about the gravity of what we were about to face.

Heavy footsteps coming down the stairs interrupted our peaceful moment. I had completely forgotten about Paul. He walked into the kitchen wearing a navy blue suit and white shirt. He was well-groomed and smiling. I soon lost my appetite.

"Good morning," he sang, kissing me on the forehead. He poured himself some coffee and leaned against the counter. "It must be the country air because I haven't slept that well in ages!"

"I'm sure the scotch didn't hurt, either," I added, sarcastically.

He laughed a fake laugh while taking some bacon from my plate. I rolled my eyes, wishing him gone.

"Honey," my mom said, clearing the counter. "I hope you don't mind, but can you drive to the church with Paul? We have to pick up Mr. and Mrs. Green. Their car won't start."

"No problem, Corinne," Paul answered, wrapping an arm around my shoulders. "Liz can give me a quick tour on our way."

"Great," I said, not even trying to hide my disappointment. I knew I should insist and take my car, but I also didn't want to press the matter in front of my parents. Being alone with Paul would give me the opportunity to make it painfully clear just how over we were.

Sitting in Paul's car, feeling anxious, I couldn't wait to get out of the small box he called *Baby*.

"Paul, we really need to talk," I said, but he cut me off as if he hadn't heard me.

"Where did you go last night?"

"Last night?" I paused. "Nowhere."

I had been positive he was asleep when I had returned, but maybe he had been faking it. He was good at that.

"Come on, Liz," he said, challenging me. "Don't lie to me."

I sighed and wrestled with the last ounce of respect I had for him. I wanted him gone and out of my life, but I just couldn't bring myself to tell him what had happened between Devon and I. No matter his faults, I didn't want to hurt Paul, even though I knew it made no sense.

"I went for a walk," I lied, hoping he would drop it. We were seconds away from the church now; I could see the steeple rising over the green hill ahead of us.

"A walk?" he snickered. "In the middle of the night?"

I was growing irate with his insistence.

"Yes, a walk. Paul, you and I are not together anymore," I spoke each word slowly and carefully as if trying to explain something to a child. "It's none of your business."

"It's really amazing. You're horseback riding, you're drinking scotch, you're taking walks alone at night," he laughed. "It's like you're a completely different person out here." His tone was sarcastic and displeasing as we pulled into the Church's parking lot.

"Maybe I am a different person out here. What difference does it make?"

"None, really," he said, parking the car. "I'm sure once you're out of this shit-hole, you'll get back to normal. I like you better that way."

I looked at him, completely repelled by his words. Though in the past I had been known to call Frelighsburg a hole-in-the-earth, I now found I was growing attached to the small town—feeling protective of it in a way.

"I thought you loved the *country air*," I asked, reminding him of his choice of words.

He rolled his eyes.

"I guess you're as gullible as your parents." He laughed as he got out of the car. "You'd believe anything, wouldn't you?"

I sat still, unable to coalesce this man with the man from last night. I had known Paul was laying it on a bit thick with my parents but to have him mock them now, and me for that matter, filled me with such anger, I had to remind myself of where I was and of how I was supposed to behave.

Sure, he had always been more or less a jerk, but I had never known him to be so blatantly two-faced and mean, especially toward me. I gave him the benefit of the doubt and assumed his attitude was because I had refused to take him back. I told myself he was acting out because of his arrogance and not because of some malicious reason. I stepped out of the car, taking a deep breath and walked over to him, brushing away his outstretched hand.

"Paul, I need you to open your ears once and for all," I ordered. "What I do, where I go and whether or not I am myself is of no damn concern of yours."

"Lizzie, calm down, people are watching," he said, looking genuinely concerned with the attention I was attracting.

"Good, let them watch." I noticed the on-lookers but paid no mind to them. Before joining my parents at the church's entrance, I turned one last time to shout, "By the way, it's Elle, not Lizzie!"

CHAPTER TWENTY-SIX

The church was filled to maximum capacity. People who couldn't find pews to sit in were left standing at the back. I had not been in this church for a long time and thought back to the last time I had been within its walls.

It was for Christmas mass and I must have been twelve or thirteen. Ironically, it had been my grandmother who had dragged me there when all I wanted to do was sleep off my turkey coma. She had forced me to sit next to her and listen to the priest drone on and on. My parents had never shared her religious beliefs, and by extension, neither had I. And though I had appreciated the choir and the lighting that lent a certain beautifully esoteric quality to things, I had never returned to the church with her again after that night. It was a touchy topic and we had shared a few arguments about it, and even if she had never truly accepted my beliefs, she did eventually respect them.

Now, as I walked down the aisle to the front of the church, ironically toward the same pew I had sat in that Christmas, my heart drummed loudly in my chest as I fought back tears.

"Just as she'd have wanted it," my dad commented, "Standing room only."

He smiled reassuringly as he took my hand. We found our

seats, accepting handshakes and condolences as we walked by. I glanced to the back and noticed Paul entering through the opened doors, hesitating. Maybe he was thinking of joining us, but thought better of it and instead stayed where he was.

Pastor Marcoux, a young and kind-looking man, stepped up to the lectern and began to address the crowd.

"Good morning," he said, the congregation quieting down. "We are here today to pay our respects to a wonderful woman, a sister to us all, Mrs. Dolores Williams. It is truly befitting of her grandeur to have you all here today, for we are all aware that to know Dolores was to indeed love her."

I looked around and saw that nearly everyone was crying and nodding their heads in agreement. The pastor continued.

"We are also here today to show our love and support for her family, the ones dearest to her heart: her only son Alexander, his wife Corinne and their daughter, Elizabeth."

I felt everyone's eyes on us, making my emotions rise up. My father's grip on my hand tightened. I squeezed his hand back.

"Not only are we all individually feeling our own grief over Dolores' passing, but our hearts sympathize with the Williams' family. I hope we can all, in our own respectful way, show them that they are not alone during this difficult time."

He paused before continuing.

"It is said that the measure of a life is not its duration but in its donation. Therefore, it is important that when we all think back on what Dolores contributed to this community, to her friends, and to her family, we remember that we have much to be thankful for. That being said, we will now hear from the ones closest to her who have come here today in hopes of sharing their memories."

Father Marcoux stepped down from the lectern and took a seat beside it. A few friends and employees stepped up to say their goodbyes, recounting their own personal and heartfelt stories. The emotion in the room felt thick, and I could feel it gnawing at me as my mother handed me a tissue. It was bittersweet to see the impact my grandmother had had on this town and on each individual. In some selfish way, I had never given much thought to how important she had been to others. She had been surrounded by so much love, a fact that relieve my grief a little but also made me miss her even more.

"Goodness, he is handsome," an elderly lady behind me quietly said to her friend.

The random comment made me glance over my shoulder. Devon made his way up to the pulpit. He looked solemn, dressed in a dark grey suit, his white shirt's top button undone. Around me, I saw many different women of various ages perk up as he addressed the room. I had known he would be here, obviously, and even though I thought I was prepared, his presence made me incredibly nervous.

"Good morning," he said, smiling as everyone replied in unison. "Dolores always knew how to fill a room, didn't she?" He laughed lightly, the sound breaking the sombre mood. "As I'm sure most of you know, I have worked for Dolores for a long time and she was there for me during the most difficult period in my life."

He looked at his sister, sitting in the first row, and she smiled back, with a nod. "Luckily for me," he continued, "she kept me from a very dark place. Though I am not a deep believer in all this," he pointed behind him to the large, emaciated effigy of Jesus, "I am sure we can all agree that she was here to help us in any way she could."

The congregation agreed with an audible sound.

"Personally, I know that even with her gone, she is still affecting my life; bringing good things and good people into it." He looked directly at me before continuing. "She has taught me that sometimes good things are few and far between and when we stumble on them it is important not to let them slip through our hands."

I heard sniffles all around me, but couldn't look away from Devon. His eyes were locked on mine and I wondered how much of that speech was about my grandmother and how much was meant for me.

"We miss you, Dolores," Devon added, finally diverting his

eyes away from mine, "But we know that you are still hanging around, making sure we don't fuck up."

He winked at me, making me smile. I saw Father Marcoux shake his head and laugh. Devon walked past me, stopping for a moment to place his hand on my shoulder. He squeezed it softly, reassuringly.

Before I knew what I was doing, my cheek was on his hand, feeling his warmth. I was already teetering in a sea of calm and torment, and so I didn't look at him as he returned to his seat, not trusting how I would react.

When the service was over, my parents and I led the congregation outside, walking solemnly across the grass to the cemetery. I knew it was unavoidable, but I was still secretly desperate to find a way out of seeing the coffin being lowered into the ground.

We took our seats, sitting on hard, metal folding chairs, my parents holding each other. I tried to stop but I couldn't help but stare into the large hole that was waiting to welcome my grandmother's body. Fighting the urge to throw up, I kept wishing I could be anywhere but there.

The weather had taken a turn and I now sat chilled, wishing I had worn something warmer than my thin cotton cardigan. My father, always the gentleman, had wrapped his jacket around my mother. I could see him shiver a little but refuse my mother's offer to give it back to him.

Suddenly, someone sat in the empty chair next to me. Without looking up, I recognized the solidity of his body, leaving me no doubt as to who it belonged to.

"How are you doing?" Devon asked, his voice warming me from the inside out.

I felt as if he wanted to wrap his arm around me but thought better of it.

"Alright," I lied. "At least I didn't have to speak."

Devon let his hand rest on my knee, slightly open as if it was an invitation for me to hold it. I hesitated at first, not wanting to give the wrong impression, but my emotions were starting to get the best of me and I felt the need to hold onto something. I placed my hand in his and felt his fingers lace themselves through mine, filling me with that familiar sense of security.

Then, the pastor read a short passage from the Bible, but I heard nothing of what he was saying. My mind was too filled with commotion. The priest soon stepped aside and let Valerie take his place.

She unfolded a small piece of paper, her hands shaking ever so slightly. She cleared her throat and began to read:

"Why cry for a soul set free? Miss me a little, but not too long and not with your head bowed low."

I felt Devon's hand squeeze mine. I looked up and saw his eyes were filled with pain.

"When you are lonely and sick of heart, go to the friends we know and bury your sorrows. Miss me but let me go."

Valerie finished reading, folding her paper up and started to cry, bringing everyone else to tears—even me. Devon's hand tightened on mine. Though I had heard the words before, the poem echoed my loss and the gravity of the situation hit me. A small sob escaped my mouth as if a cork had been removed from a bottle.

They began to lower the coffin, painfully slowly, and I could feel my heart constricting like someone was squeezing it tight with their hand. The tears came pouring out and I found I was unable to stop them. My mother handed me a tissue, but I knew it would be useless.

Devon's arm was around me within seconds, as he pulled me to my feet and led me away from the crowd. I was embarrassed by my sudden lack of self-control but was relieved to have him near me, that he'd had the predilection to take me away from there. We walked through the tombstones, as far from everyone as we could get and sat down on a bench.

"I thought I could keep it together," I said in between sobs. "I'm sorry."

"Why are you apologizing?" he said, placing his unoccupied hand on mine. I shook my head, unsure why I felt guilty for showing grief. "You have every right to be sad, Elle. And this is the one place people won't think you're nuts if you cry in public."

"I suppose," I laughed, wiping away tears. "Beautiful eulogy, by the way. She would have loved it."

I wanted to ask what his inspiration had been, if any part of what he had said was directed at me, but chose to remain quiet.

"Thanks, I meant every word of it. It came to me last night, ironically, out of nowhere. As if she'd been there, whispering the words in my ear." He smiled and looked away.

I followed his stare and saw the names inscribed on a large, granite tombstone—*David and Micheline Barrett*. Devon's parents. I tightened my grip on his hand.

"The tulips are beautiful," I said, seeing the newly bloomed white flowers planted by the grave marker.

"Valerie plants them every year."

"Do you come often?"

He shook his head, frowning. "Not as much as I should."

"They're not really here, though, are they? So I guess that's OK."

"I guess."

I leaned my head on his shoulder, feeling him kiss my hair.

"Thank you, Devon, for being with me this weekend. I don't think I could have handled all of this without you." I felt the weight lifting off my chest as I spoke. "I know it's all ending, but I just wanted you to know, to understand, how important it was to me. How grateful I am."

"It's all ending, is it?"

Someone behind us cleared their throat and I felt a pit in my gut. We both turned around, my fears confirmed.

"What are you still doing here?" I shouted, dropping Devon's hand.

"Who's this guy?" Paul asked, ignoring me. Sticking out his chest, he resembled an animated cartoon character.

Devon stood up and offered his hand, introducing himself, apparently unbothered by Paul's interruption.

"Hi, I'm Devon Barrett. I'm a family friend."

I watched the two men sizing each other up and couldn't help but notice that as tall as Paul was, Devon was slightly taller. Paul seemed aware of that fact and stretched his body a little bit more.

"Family friend?" Paul replied, condescendingly. "If you're such a good *friend*, then why has she never mentioned you?"

"Not sure," Devon said, giving Paul a once-over. "Then again, she's never mentioned *you*, either."

"Oh, yeah?" Paul countered as if he was rearing for a fight.

I couldn't take it anymore.

"Guys, stop. Paul, you really should leave."

"It's fine, Elle. I've got to go, anyway," Devon said, ignoring Paul. He turned to me, "I'm going to stop by the stables before heading to the reception."

I nodded and forced a smile, knowing how hard the rest of this day would be.

"I'll see you there."

"Stables?" Paul snickered, as Devon walked past him. "You work with horses? You're a stable boy?"

I heard the condescension in his tone, his face smug, overwhelming me with the intense desire to smack him.

Stepping closer to Paul, Devon grinned. "You would assume that, wouldn't you? Actually, no Paul, I *own* horses."

Devon walked away, beaming with confidence and pride, and I couldn't help but smile. Paul shook his head and tried to act unphased, but I could tell he had definitely been put in his place.

"Interesting," he eventually said once we were alone. He laughed a sardonic laugh. "It all makes so much sense now. He's why you suddenly like horseback riding so much?"

"I'm warning you. Drop it."

"Well, I hope he at least gave you a good ride."

Abruptly, my hand made contact with his face. I had never slapped anyone before, and though I could feel the sting on my palm, I had to admit that I felt invigorated.

"Get the fuck out of here, Paul." I was poking him in the chest, forcing him to walk backward. "How dare you come here and ruin my grandmother's funeral. Go! Leave!"

"Come on, I'm not going anywhere until we have a talk."

"What the hell do you and I have to talk about anymore?" I realized I was shouting and knew I was attracting some attention from the people nearby. "This isn't the time or the place."

"Then I'll wait," he said. "I am sure your parents would love for me to stick around."

I looked at him, incredulous.

"Damn it, Paul, why are you being such a—"

"—If Ellie says you're no longer welcomed, then maybe you should listen to her," my mother said, appearing out of nowhere. She wrapped her arm around me. "Why don't you go home, Peter."

"It's Paul," he corrected, offended.

"Right," my mom replied. "It doesn't really matter, does it? Now, fuck off."

Looking insulted, his ego clearly bruised and attempting to save face, Paul turned and left without another word. I watched him get into his car and speed away; wondering if this time it would finally be for good.

"Mom, that wasn't very polite."

I tried to seem genuinely concerned, but couldn't stop from grinning. She shrugged and kissed me on the head. "You deserve better, Elizabeth."

CHAPTER TWENTY-SEVEN

I walked with my parents down the street to the restaurant where the reception was to be held. *Le Ruisseau* was the town's go-to place for terrific French cuisine. It was also run by my parent's friends, Roger and Marie, and so naturally, it had been offered as the place to hold the funeral reception.

The quaint and romantic bistro-style restaurant was now packed with far too many people, all of them mingling and drinking. Most of the tables had been moved out of the way, only a few were left on the perimeter of the dining room.

I mingled as much as possible, trying to ignore the troubled feeling I felt deep down. I spoke to people I didn't even know, keeping an eye on the door for Devon, wondering where he was and when he would stop by. A part of me secretly wished he wouldn't show up—if only to make my leaving less painful. I hadn't thought so far as to when I would leave town, but now that it was lingering closely, I started to feel more and more anxious about it. I hated goodbyes, and now with my decision set and finalized in my mind—as much as it would ever be—I was dreading having to talk about it with Devon. But I knew I had to.

I went to the bar and ordered a drink—a gin and tonic this

time—I needed something a little stronger to settle my nerves. I looked around, trying to find somewhere to sit and get some time with my thoughts but soon realized that privacy wasn't remotely possible in such cramped quarters.

Finding a small two-seater table at the back windows, near the kitchen, I sat down with my drink and watched the river streaming down below. Alone with my thoughts, I hadn't even heard Nicole approach me.

"Mind if I sit down?" she asked. Not bothering to wait for my answer, she pulled out a chair.

"Go right ahead," I said, trying to stay polite but feeling rather annoyed.

Great, this won't be awkward at all.

"How are you doing, Ellie?" she asked, directly. There wasn't any sign of empathy in her tone.

"I'm fine," I answered. I looked around to see if there was any escaping. "You?"

"I've been better," she was serious. "It was a beautiful service, wasn't it?"

Her question surprised me. I had assumed this was where she would confront me like she had at the bar. I wasn't in the mood for conflict, especially not under current circumstances, surrounded by so many prying ears.

"It was."

I was trying desperately to keep a calm demeanour and forget the ice in her stare the last time I had seen her. There was a quiet pause between us, both of us seeming uncomfortable and uncertain who would speak first.

"Listen, about Devon," she finally began.

"Nicole, not here," I interrupted. "Please. Can we talk about this someplace else?"

"I don't think so," she said, lowering her voice to a whisper. "It's really important that I say this. Now."

I shook my head not wanting to hear it. I couldn't believe she was choosing this moment to say whatever she was about to. I had just laid my grandmother to rest. Didn't she have any respect for her?

"Look," I snapped. "I know it's complicated between the two of you and I'm not trying to get in between."

She giggled, catching me off guard. It wasn't at all the reaction I was expecting.

"See, that's the thing," she said, leaning over the table, getting closer. "You are between us now."

"Then maybe you should talk to Devon about this," I replied, pushing my chair back and standing up, exasperated and honestly, a little bit scared.

"I have." She grabbed my wrist. "Please sit down. Just give me one minute. It's important."

I hesitated, breathing hard, my heart racing. I looked around and was saw no one seemed to be paying us any attention. Reluctantly, I sat back down.

"I've spoken to Devon about all this and that's why I'm talking to you now. He called me last night after you left his place."

I sat back, stunned. *How could he have called her after spending hours with me?* Images of Devon sharing details about our private time together filled my mind, but I said nothing and let her continue.

"I've never heard him talk the way he did, Ellie. He seems really taken by you."

I shook my head in disbelief, about to cut her off, when she continued.

"Despite what you might think, I'm not out to get you, Ellie. I'm not such a horrible person."

"I never said you were," I said, trying to sound convincing, but I could hear the uncertainty in my voice.

"Maybe not to my face, but I'm not stupid. I know you don't like me, and that's fine. But I care about Devon and I want him to be happy. And as much as I wish him and I had a future, the things he said to me last night prove that we don't."

Curiosity was killing me. I wanted to know what he had said, but I was also glad she wasn't about to share. I felt that hearing how Devon felt would just make everything that much harder. Besides, I was pretty sure I already knew.

"I'm sorry, Nicole. I wish things were different for you two."

"No you don't, but thanks, I appreciate that," she said, sipping on her drink. "Can I ask what you plan to do with him?"

"Do with him?"

"You don't seem to keen on this going any further than it has."

"Why would I want it to go any further?"

She looked at me sideways with a grin. "You can't see it, can you?"

"See what?"

My heart was in my throat and I knew exactly what she was about to say. My leg began to fidget beneath the table, my nerves increasing. I kept hoping she would just leave and stop talking. I knew she wouldn't, though.

"How crazy he is about you."

Great, she'd said it.

I shook my head. "It's just a crush. It's a challenge to him."

"A challenge?"

"Yeah," I explained, keeping my composure as best I could. "It's a game. The distance between us, the fact that it can't work, that piques his interest. Let's face it. If I lived here and if he saw me every day, then I'm sure it would fade."

"Wow," she said, laughing. "And here I thought you were a smart girl. The man is falling in love with you but you can't see it. That's really sad."

"I think you're the one seeing things."

"What I see is that I wish he felt one-tenth for me what he feels for you," she said, taking a sip of her mimosa, gauging my reaction. I remained as neutral as I could, letting her words sink in. "But if you truly aren't interested then that's good news for me."

"Why are you even telling me this?" I asked, my anger spilling over. "If you still care for him so much, wouldn't it be better if I left town without knowing this."

"Trust me, I've considered that." She turned in her chair

and looked me in the eye. "But, above everything else, I just want him to be happy. And if it's not with me, then so be it."

I doubted her altruism. She appeared to be honest and well-meaning, but still, though I tried to stop myself, I laughed just the same.

"I'll think about it," I replied, between giggles.

She nodded, stood up and walked away. And just like that, our conversation was over.

My drink was sitting on the table, untouched. I drank it all as quickly as I could, feeling the alcohol burn my throat. I looked around at the crowd. The restaurant had filled up a little more since I had shown up. The room was easily filled with a hundred people or more, and yet, I never felt more alone.

I checked in on my parents who were in much higher spirits than they had been that morning. Several times I caught them lovingly embrace. It comforted me knowing that at least they had each other to help with their grief. Seeing them together, chatting with friends, I thought that maybe this would be the best time to leave. I was horrible at goodbyes and this one wouldn't be any different, of that I was sure. The idea of having to say farewell to them this time around felt like an impossible feat—one that I would gladly avoid if I were given the choice.

I was headed for the exit when I locked eyes with those impenetrable green eyes on the other side of the double doors.

"Where are you headed?" Devon asked, shutting the door behind him, positioning himself between me and freedom.

I felt relief and anxiety hit me at the exact same moment. As much as I had craved his company an hour earlier, now, with Nicole's words so fresh in my brain, I felt scared, even more so than he usually made me feel.

"Home," I replied, attempting to walk around him.

"Really? But I just got here," he said, looking disappointed.

"You can stay."

He moved aside allowing me to push the door open. Nearly bursting out of the stifling restaurant, I felt tears bubbling up and desperately didn't want him to see me crying.

"Elle, wait up."

I stopped in my steps and caught sight of a few onlookers outside for a smoke.

"Where's Paul?" he asked and I noted the contempt in his voice.

"Gone," I replied, the fact bringing me a morsel of comfort.

"And how are you getting home?" he asked.

I shrugged. "I didn't think that far ahead. He was my ride, so I guess I'll walk."

He shook his head and put an arm around my waist.

"Let me give you a ride."

I looked around, considering my options. The walk home would be several kilometres and I was in no physical shape to make that walk.

I knew I shouldn't get in his car, and that it would only lead to the inevitable but I knew I couldn't ignore it anymore and that it had to be dealt with, once and for all.

CHAPTER TWENTY-EIGHT

When we pulled up to my parents' house, I was in full panic. I knew very well Devon wasn't going to just leave me alone, no matter what I said to him. He would want to know what had happened with Paul and why he had caught me in the middle of an attempted getaway. Inside, the house felt cold and dark. We walked into the living room in total silence.

"Drink?" I offered, moving to the bar. Hesitating at first, I chose the bottle of *Blue Label* —this would require the good stuff.

"To Grandma." We clinked our glasses. I sat down in a nearby chair, sipping my drink, nervously.

"What's going on, Elle?" He sat down across from me, leaning back. "Did Paul do something?"

I shook my head. "No, nothing like that."

Taking another sip, he watched me over the rim of his glass. His green eyes were piercing, impatient. I could sense he was waiting for me to say something but seemed patient enough to let me gather my thoughts.

"Might as well get it over with, then." I inhaled deep and swallowed hard. "I made a decision."

He sat up, his attention caught.

"A decision? That's great."

He seemed so relieved it almost made what I was about to say that much more painful. I could see the anticipation in his eyes, the expectation he was unaware I was about to crush.

"Don't get too excited, it's probably not what you're thinking." His smile vanished, replaced with confusion. "Before I tell you what I've decided I want you to know that this past couple of days with you have been..."

"Sublime," he said as if reading my thoughts.

"Yes, sublime." I could feel myself blushing, the room feeling suddenly very warm. "And I want to thank you for showing me such a great time and for being there for me. It's helped me, a lot." He shook his head and looked away, embarrassed. "I've thought long and hard about this and there is no possible way for me to take over the business, at least not alone."

His head bolted up, his eyes meeting mine.

"What do you mean?"

"It will still technically be mine, on paper, but I won't be the one running it."

He tilted his head as if he already knew what I was about to say.

"You want me to run it."

"Yes. You'll take over where Dolores left off. You've been the closest to her and already know how everything works. If I got involved now, I'd just mess it up, I'm sure."

I smiled at him, hoping against hope he would see it my way and know it was the smartest way to go about all this. But in the short amount of time we'd spent together, I had a feeling that would be easier said than done.

"I see," was all he said.

Clearly, I had expected a little more from him than what he was giving me, so I continued talking, my words sounding forced as if I was trying desperately to make him agree with me.

"It really makes the most sense. You'll keep doing what you're doing, but with a higher paycheck." I giggled, but he still wasn't reacting. He was starring off somewhere, his thoughts far away from our present conversation. "Devon? Aren't you going to say anything?"

"What do you want me to say?"

"I don't know, anything. A *thank you* would work, too."

His eyes shot to meet mine and I could tell something was brewing beneath his calm exterior. I saw a flash of anger and expected him to burst out yelling any second.

Instead, he smiled at me, his grin not reaching his eyes. "Thank you."

There was no honesty behind his words. Silence fell as I struggled to figure out what to say next. I couldn't understand why he was suddenly being so reserved, so distant.

"The more I've thought about it, the more I realized that the entire reason I am even here is that Dolores wanted it this way. And no matter which scenario I put myself in, inevitably I feel wrong about giving the business to someone else, even my father. Since you're the only person who seems to be as emotionally invested in the orchards as she was, I think she'd more than agree this is the right thing to do."

He nodded slowly, his eyes not leaving mine, but still, he said nothing.

I snapped, feeling annoyed and hurt. "I don't get it. Why aren't you happy about this?"

"I am happy, Ellie," he said, walking to the bar. helping himself to another drink. "After all, this was your decision. If you're happy with it, then so am I." He took a big gulp of his drink, nearly downing the entire thing. He then took a long breath and as if he was convincing himself to, he spoke again. "I'm just wondering why you are so afraid?"

"Afraid? Of what? I'm not afraid."

"Where do I start? Afraid of what could happen between you and me. What *has* happened."

"I'm not afraid of that. And I've given it a lot of thought, Devon. I know we can't be together and work with each other, it—"

"It won't work. Yeah, you've established that. I'm not just

talking about us. You're afraid of being a success here and afraid of dealing with your past. You've told yourself that you can't make this work so much that you won't even try. Once again, you're running away because you're afraid. And if you want to keep doing that, then do it. I won't stop you. But maybe you should see it for what it is and take a damn chance."

"You don't know what you're talking about. I'd make a mess of it. You don't know me, but I would."

"I think I know you well enough by now and I can clearly see you've got issues."

"Thanks, Devon. This is just what I needed to hear right now."

"Maybe you don't want to hear it, but you should. You need to let it go, Elle. Your parents, whatever happened, it's over. Your grandmother thought you could handle this and if you think so highly of her then maybe you should give her more credit. You are incredibly strong but you have no idea."

I rolled my eyes, fighting back tears.

He didn't know me.

He continued, "You've been given a chance that most would dream of and you're just going to pass it along like it's not worth it."

"It's not that simple. But it doesn't matter what you think right now. It's my decision and all you need to tell me is if you'll go along with it or not."

"Ellie, it is that simple. Can't you see it? You're letting your insecurities mess up whatever chance you have here."

"I'm not insecure!" He looked at me with what I could only describe as a mix of annoyance and pity. It struck me hard. "I'm not, Devon. And if you think that, then you really don't know me at all."

"Fine, I guess I'm wrong."

"You are." I took a breath, steadying my shaky nerves. "You're completely wrong," I added as if I needed to drive the point home a little more. I was starting to feel my exterior crumble. "When I get home I'll figure out what needs to be done exactly. This is all new to me, so I'd appreciate it if you gave me some time to settle all the details and whatnot."

"Sure," he replied, resigned. "Take all the time you need."

I was fuming but tried to keep my composure steady. I had been so worried that this conversation would be awkward; instead, it had turned into something incredibly emotional and draining. I was hurt that he thought so little of me and I was disappointed that everything had taken a turn for the worse. I could feel my emotions bubble and I knew I needed to end this now. If he didn't leave soon, I would find it impossible to keep everything together.

"That's all I wanted to say."

His lips parted as if he was about to speak but then he closed them again. He slammed his glass on the bar top, making me cringe, and walked over to me. My heart was beating so loudly, I was sure he would be able to hear it. I closed my eyes, desperately grasping on to whatever self-control I had left, which wasn't much. I felt I would soon be unable to hold back my tears.

He leaned down, placing his hands on the chair, his arms on either side of me, boxing me in. His face was now so close to mine, I could smell the alcohol on his breath. He stared at me for a moment, his eyes searching mine. Then, he moved in close and kissed me softly on the cheek, grazing the corner of my mouth. I felt my walls crumble but kept my eyes shut so he wouldn't see my world caving in.

"Take care, Elizabeth," he said, mere inches from my face.

His steps walking away echoed through the large, empty house. The sound of the door slamming shut made me wince. Though it took me a few minutes before I could trust myself to reopen my eyes, once I did, the tears fell as if they were making up for lost time.

It was all for the best, that much I knew, but no matter how many times I repeated it to myself, the pain inside never ceased.

Curling up in the chair, unable to move, I tucked my head into my lap and let myself cry.

Later, I heard my parents come home.

I had no idea how long I'd been sitting in the dark, empty living room, but I figured it had been a long while.

"She's in here," my father said, walking in, turning the lights on. My eyes had become used to the dark and the brightness made me squint. "We were wondering where you'd disappeared to. How long have you been here?"

"Why were you sitting in the dark?" my mother asked, her voice filled with concern.

She sat down beside me and rubbed my back.

"I've been thinking," I said, my voice feeble.

My parents took in my appearance, my face covered in tears.

"What the hell happened?" my father yelled, clearly jumping to conclusions. "Did someone hurt you?"

"No, Dad. Don't worry about it," I reassured him. "I'm going to bed."

My mother placed a hand on my shoulder and left it there for a moment. She smiled at me, sympathetic. With all the will I could muster, I returned the smile, even though no part of me felt in the vicinity of happiness.

Reaching my bed, the weight of the day's pressure finally caught up with me. I fell onto it, exhausted. My last waking moments were spent wondering why everything that had made so much sense earlier in the day, now felt wholly and fundamentally wrong?

Monday, April 24th

CHAPTER TWENTY-NINE

My brain had been taken over by a jackhammer that was working overtime, that's what I told myself when I opened my eyes. By far worse than any hangover I had ever suffered, my eyes were red and painful, and my face was puffy from crying so much.

Grudgingly, I went downstairs to meet my parents in the kitchen. They were speaking in hushed tones, either to avoid waking me or because they didn't want me overhearing. The moment I entered the room they immediately went quiet. They looked at me with pity, making me feel guilty. I had been right the previous day—I should have gone back to the city and avoided all of this.

"Good morning," my mother said, handing me a cup of coffee. "Did you get any sleep?"

I winced in response, taking a slow sip. The warmth felt good going down but my head kept pounding away.

"A few hours, maybe," I lied, not wanting her to feel worse for me. I didn't know why she was being so nice to me, but I assumed that the argument we'd had the other night was now water under the bridge.

"Honey," my father began. "If you're feeling up to it..."

I watched him hesitate and my mother cleared her throat.

"Say it," I snapped.

"We were just wondering what your plan is for the house? But we can talk about it another time if you'd rather."

Ironically, the decision regarding my grandmother's house had been the easiest part of this entire weekend.

I took a deep breath.

"I get why Grandma was angry with Mom, but the way I see it, if you've both moved on, then there is no valid reason to keep it from you. The house is rightfully yours. She should have seen that. I'll transfer the ownership as soon as I can."

My mother looked away, but I could see tears in her eyes. She reached for my hand and squeezed it tight.

"Thank you, Elizabeth," she said, smiling.

I wasn't sure if it was because she was crying, or because she hadn't smiled at me in what seemed like forever, but I felt my own surge of heartache rising up.

"You're welcome," I replied, clearing my throat. "But you'll let me know if you need any help clearing out Grandma's stuff?"

I wasn't entirely sure I'd be of any real help, but I felt I should offer. Plus, the idea of coming back home any time in the near future wasn't exactly high on my list of priorities.

"Absolutely." My mother smiled again, filled with what looked like surprise and doubt.

"Good."

I peered out the windows at the pristine lake. To think only a week ago none of this was even a speck in my imagination. Now, here I was land and business owner, both of which I wasn't remotely interested in being. And to top it off, I was also broken-hearted and growing unhappier every minute more I spent in Frelighsburg.

I looked at the time and thought now was the perfect opportunity to leave. The previous night had turned into such a disaster, and since I had stayed the night, I felt in even more of a rush to get home.

"I should get going."

"Sweetie, you are more than welcomed to stay a couple

more days," my mother suggested. "It might do you good."

"I sincerely doubt that, Mom." Though the idea of driving home with everything so fresh in my mind was less than appealing, I knew it was a safer option than sticking around town, next door to Devon, for much longer. "Thanks, but I need to get home. I've got work and my neighbour was expecting me last night."

"Right," my mom said, probably finding my excuse as lame as I did.

Once I had packed my things, my dad carried my bag to the car while I stayed back with my mom.

"Ellie, I know there are a lot of things you and I need to talk about," she said. "I understand you may not want to, but I would really like the chance to sit down with you one day and talk things out."

Her offer was so surprising. She was barely recognizable to me any longer. In the span of a few days, she had become kinder, more soft-spoken. I didn't know for sure, but I thought that maybe my grandmother's passing had shaken something deep down inside of her.

"That would be nice," I said, hugging her. "I'll call you, Mom."

My father hugged me and kissed me goodbye.

"Drive safe," was all he said to me as I got in the car.

I drove by Devon's house and couldn't stop myself from looking toward it. There was so much I wanted to say to him but knew it was probably better left unsaid. For some strange reason, I couldn't help but glance in the rear-view mirror in hopes of possibly seeing him. It was silly, I knew, but again, the eternal romantic in me just couldn't let go.

Walking up the two flights of stairs to my apartment, I found Mrs. Benson waiting for me.

"Max got into the garbage a few times, but I cleaned it all

up really well," she said, handing me my keys.

I unlocked the door and peeked into my apartment. The apartment was spotless, even cleaner than I had left it. I was sure Mrs. Benson had cleaned up more than she was letting on.

"Thank you," I replied, handing her some money, which she refused.

"By the way, a nice-looking young man came by the other day. Asking where you were. I believe he said his name was Paul," Mrs. Benson said, sweetly.

I nodded, disappointed and bit my tongue.

"Yes, he found me. Thank you."

"I'm sure it's none of my business, my dear, but I don't like the looks of that man," she added, grimacing. "I think you could do better."

I found it impossible not to laugh and I thanked her once more. Her words reminded me of how my mother had said the same thing at the funeral. I didn't know what they saw in me that made them think that way.

Settling back into my apartment, I threw my bag into my bedroom. I looked in my fridge, not remotely hungry, but needing something to fill the lonely void. My choices were some mouldy cheese or ancient leftovers. Deciding I would need to go to the store at some point, I shut the refrigerator door and turned the TV on.

I glanced at my laptop. The nagging voice in my head had returned with a vengeance, and despite knowing that I should give myself more time, I turned it on. My fingers hovered over the keys, the words still forming in my brain.

What on earth could I say?

Taking a deep breath, I began to type:

Devon,
I wanted to say that I am sorry for how things ended. Please know I never meant to hurt you or to cause any trouble. I hope in time you'll understand and come to see things from my side. In the meantime, no matter how you feel about this, we will still need to work together. That being said, should any problems come up, please do not hesitate to contact me. Here's hoping we can be grown-ups about this.
Yours, Elle

I hesitated before sending the email, reading it over and over again. My mind felt heavy from all the thoughts weighing on it but they weren't things I could very well share over email. I had to accept the way things were.

Eventually, I pressed *Send* and turned the laptop off.

Max emerged from his hiding spot and curled up beside me, purring and rubbing his head against my arm. I welcomed the warmth and familiarity of him while I scratched his head. As if struck by the extent of everything that had happened over the weekend, my body became heavy and I was overcome with such an incredible fatigue, I could barely keep my eyes open. I reached for the blanket hanging over the side of the sofa—one knitted by my grandmother—and tucked myself in, resting my head on a cushion. The television was blasting images at me, but I wasn't watching them. The sounds masked the beating of my heart. My eyes became blurry and I realized it was from tears. Though Max kept purring as he nuzzled up beside me, I felt cold and alone.

"Well, Max," I said, my voice sounding harsh and gruff. "I really fucked it up this time, didn't I?"

Friday, May 26th

CHAPTER THIRTY

Over a month had gone by since that eventful weekend and I slowly settled back into my old routine. Work had picked up and I had received a few more contracts to work on—nothing fancy but it was enough to keep my mind occupied. It was just what I needed to feel like things were back to how they should be.

At least that's what I kept telling myself.

Devon had kept his word, at least. Throughout the weeks, our communications were rare and usually only focused on financial spreadsheets he was nice enough to walk me through. Nothing major had happened or needed to be decided, so he didn't need to contact me more than necessary.

It became clear to me that the entire world of business was well above my pay grade and I was glad that I had left it in Devon's capable hands. The way I saw it, so long as our email exchanges remained silent, I assumed the business was running smoothly and that meant I wouldn't need to do much if anything at all.

Still, I constantly felt like I was dropping the ball. I imagined I wasn't exactly living up to my grandmother's expectations. I doubted my decision, thinking I should be working alongside Devon, after all, taking a little more responsibility.

In hopes of figuring out how to be an entrepreneur in the quickest time possible, I checked out some books from the library—mainly Business for Dummies-type books—which led me to enrol in a business night class. It was much tougher than I had imagined, but I knew I needed to do it if only to understand a little more of what I was responsible for. But it was all so very, very boring.

I was in the middle of reading a chapter about the relationship between marketing and sales, forcing my eyes to stay open, when my phone rang. It was my mom. I rolled my eyes, putting the book down. It seemed like she was calling me quite a bit these days. Though this newfound closeness between her and I was something I hadn't known I was missing, a part of me hated the emotions our conversations would inevitably bring up.

Also, it seemed like all we ever talked about lately was her plans for my grandmother's house. My parents had decided to turn Dolores' home into a bed and breakfast, something that was strangely lacking in Frelighsburg. The town's popularity was growing among tourists and there was definitely a market for it. Surprisingly to me, my parents had asked Valerie to help out and be the manager once it was open.

"It's so much work but it will be well worth it," my mother said, and I could hear the joy in her voice. "Maybe you could come and see it, once we're all done. You know, before the wedding."

Ah, the wedding. A few days prior, I had received an invitation in the mail—cream-coloured and rimmed in gold—to Brian and Mark's wedding in September. It had a rushed look to it as if they had decided to invite me as a courtesy more than anything, so I had thrown the invitation aside. I had assumed I wouldn't even bother going, but strangely the thought had started growing on me.

"I don't know, Mom," I said, hesitation in my voice. "I'll see."

Lately, she had been skirting the topic but hadn't fully said it until now. I knew she wanted me to visit—or maybe more—but no matter how much I told her it wasn't going to happen, she clearly wasn't planning on letting it go.

"Fine, fine," she said, giving up the fight for the moment. She quickly changed the subject. "You should see the trees, though. The orchard is doing great this year. It's so full."

I smiled, filled with unexpected pride. Though I hadn't felt much attachment to the orchard before, since my return home, I had started to feel more excited when I heard how well it was doing. And with its continued success under Devon's experienced hands, I found I wasn't completely averse to hearing about it.

"That's good to hear. It must be beautiful."

I could imagine the trees blossoming, the leaves and flowers turning the orchard into a true sight to see.

"Absolutely beautiful."

She was quiet for a moment and I knew there was more she wasn't saying.

"What is it?"

"Oh, nothing," she lied.

"Mom..."

"Alright," she said, taking in a deep breath, steadying herself for what she was about to say. "I know you don't like to talk about it. But really, he looks horrible."

I knew immediately who she meant and felt my stomach drop.

"You're right; I don't want to talk about it."

"Don't you miss him?" She had brought up the subject a few times over the past weeks, and my answer had always been the same. She knew this, yet she always insisted. "He doesn't talk to me about it, but I can tell—the man is broken."

"I'm sure you believe that, but I doubt it's true."

There was a part of me that wanted to believe her. I wanted to know that this was as difficult for Devon as it was for me. However, I knew it was probably my mother's flagrant imagination getting the best of her.

"Elizabeth, don't do that. Don't underestimate your value."

I rolled my eyes, truly not interested in discussing my self-esteem with my mother.

"I'm not underestimating, Mom. Whatever happened between him and me is in the past. Besides, I'm his boss now. It's better this way."

"You know I wholeheartedly disagree with that. I think if you just—,"

"No, Mom. Drop it," I interrupted sharply. "I have to go. We'll talk soon. Bye."

Before giving her the chance to speak again, I hung up. The fact was I was finally accepting the working relationship I had with Devon and in the limited times we had spoken, it was via email. The distance made it so much easier to forget how I felt, what we had done and what I had given up.

The truth remained—and I hated admitting it—I did miss him. Horribly. I missed the way he had made me feel, the way he could bring a smile to my face without even saying a word. I sincerely hoped he was busy with the company and that it required all his time and energy. I didn't want to know that instead, he was sitting around like I was, constantly sulking and desperately trying to forget what had happened. I prayed he wasn't having trouble sleeping at night like I was.

The sadness I had been trying to keep at bay started to creep back in. I attacked the fridge and opened a bottle of wine, pouring myself a rather large glass. Nudging Max aside, I sat on the sofa and turned on the TV, my constant companion these days. As per my usual nights spent alone at home, I was faced with nothing but horribly cheesy romantic comedies and post-apocalyptic zombie films. Not wanting any reminders of my failed love life, I chose the latter.

A mob of zombies was about to attack a small group of survivors when I was startled by a knock at the door. It wasn't late, but I wasn't expecting anyone either, so I proceeded cautiously. Making sure the chain was in place, I opened the door slowly, peeping through the opening.

My heart sank.

CHAPTER THIRTY-ONE

"Hi, Elle," Devon said, his voice sexy and soft.

It took me a few seconds to accept that he was, in fact, standing at my door. If at all possible, he looked even better than I remembered. He seemed tired, his eyes a little less striking than usual, but nothing that made him any less appealing. I quickly shook off the familiar feeling creeping up inside of me.

"What are you doing here?" I finally managed to say, barely more than a whisper. I noted that it came out rather rudely.

"Why don't you take that down," he suggested, pointing to the chain.

As I did what he asked, I took advantage while the door was momentarily closed to take a deep breath. When I reopened the door, I found him smiling, his bright, enchanting smile. On the television, a largely breasted red-head was running for her life from a mob of the undead. I hurried to turn it off, embarrassed.

"Can I come in?"

"Yes, of course," I said, realizing I had left him standing in the doorway.

I now saw that he was holding a large, cardboard box. I nodded toward it.

"Valerie was cleaning out Dolores' things and she found these." He handed me the box and I looked inside to see it was filled with picture frames. "She thought that maybe you'd want them. Your mother said you might."

I set the box down on the coffee table. "These are terrific. Thank you. It means a lot that you went through all this trouble."

The weight of a thousand words left unsaid weighed heavy on my chest.

"It was no trouble, really. It was my pleasure," he paused. "How have you been?"

"Good. You?"

"I've been alright."

"The orchards are doing well?"

"Really well."

The small talk was killing me and I was desperate for something less awkward or pointless to say.

"Elle, I need to say something to you," he said, breaking the tension. Hearing my name coming from those lips sent a wave of elation through me. "The last time we saw each other, what I said to you, it was inexcusable. I was being a selfish dick and I'm sorry."

A little surprised by his apology, I took a moment to let it sink in.

"I appreciate that Devon, I really do, but there's no need. It's been a while." I sat down. He approached me but didn't sit. "Either way, everything you said was true. Had you not said it, I wouldn't be here now. You were right. I have always doubted myself and sadly, no one ever cared enough to push me in the right direction. Had it not been for your words, I wouldn't have dreamt I'd be able to do what I'm doing now."

He blushed and I was relieved to finally have what I was feeling out in the open.

"You are doing a great job, as a matter of fact," Devon agreed, making me smile.

"Thanks, so are you."

I tucked a strand of hair behind my ear, trying desperately

to keep my hands busy. The silence once again filled the room and space between us. His eyes shifted toward the box and he looked as if he wanted to say more.

"Do you want a drink?" I asked, hopeful.

To my surprise, he refused. "Thanks, but I should probably get going."

"Come on, you didn't come all the way here just to bring me a box of pictures, did you?" I tried not to seem too desperate for his company, but I could tell it was in vain.

"Yeah, actually I did. I figured it would give me the chance to apologize, too."

"Oh," I replied, my disappointment obvious.

"I've got plans tonight, anyhow, so I should get going."

"Plans? Like a date?" I asked, unable to hide my surprise.

"Kind of."

It took me a moment to register his answer.

Obviously, he was dating. How long could I expect someone like him to be single? He was such a rare specimen, I was sure women were lining up to ask him out. Without a doubt, Nicole would have been the first in line.

"That's good," I lied. "Don't let me keep you, then."

We walked to the door together and stopped, the air feeling thick.

"Thank you again, Devon. It was nice seeing you."

"You're welcome, Elle."

I opened the door for him and as he walked past me, he stopped and kissed me on the cheek.

"Hope we'll see each other soon."

I nodded, my heart about to explode. He walked away down the hall and I shut the door, biting my lip to stop myself from screaming. Holding my head in my hands, I hoped that these feelings I had for him would soon vanish and that one day in the future I would be able to be around him without feeling like this.

I walked to the box and took out some pictures. Maybe the images would conjure up some happy memories, or at the very least, memories that would distract me from the gaping hole that had just been reopened in my chest. The portraits were mainly from my childhood—family picnics, birthdays, even one with my grandfather and I, canoeing on the lake. They were of happier times when secrets were non-existent and we all got along and loved one another, when there were no complications. Unlike now.

I continued rummaging through the box a little while longer, finding a picture without a frame. Worried it would get bent, I quickly took it out. Turning its face up, I nearly dropped it when I saw who was photographed. It was a black and white picture of a few people sitting around a bonfire. More importantly, it was the bonfire we'd had after my grandmother's wake. And there, in the centre of the picture were Devon and me, sitting side by side, roasting marshmallows. We were deep in conversation, completely oblivious of our picture being taken.

I could remember that moment so clearly in my mind. It was when things had officially shifted between us, and somehow the photographer, whoever they were, had captured those feelings. They had captured the intensity and the passion I had felt when looking into Devon's eyes. The same passion I had felt just a few moments ago when he'd been standing in my apartment.

And just like that, it was as if a light had turned on in the darkness that I had let grow in my heart. I bolted up, the box falling onto the couch and I ran for the door.

Maybe I wasn't too late.

I hoped against all logic that he wasn't gone yet. Running down the stairs, taking some two at a time, I reached the door, out of breath. Crashing onto the sidewalk, I looked both ways, gasping for air. People noticed me, one woman who was pushing a stroller seemed frightened, but I didn't care, especially not when I saw him there, leaning against the wall, a small grin on his face.

Relief very visibly washed over me.

"You put that picture in there, didn't you?" I asked, getting closer.

He stepped closer still, smiling coyly and shrugged.

"Maybe I did."

He took me in his arms, gently framing my face with his hands. Their warmth filled me with a feeling of safety and love that, until that moment, I hadn't realized I had missed so much.

I smiled. "You knew I'd come down, didn't you?"

"I figured it was worth a try."

Saturday, November 18th

CHAPTER THIRTY-TWO

The sun was incredibly hot; my skin feeling the slow burn, but there wasn't any chance I was leaving. We were almost at the end of our two-week vacation and I didn't even want to consider going home—not yet, anyway.

She was swimming in the pool and I got hard just watching her. It wasn't uncommon for her to have that effect on me. I found that even seeing her in her baggy pyjamas could arouse me.

There wasn't much time for pyjamas these days, though. A fact that made me particularly happy she had agreed to some time off. I was even more relieved that she let me splurge on this private retreat. We could have stayed anywhere, really, but this place, with its privacy and its complete seclusion from the world, well, let's just say it was conducive to the things we had been doing during our trip. It amused me to no end how she always seemed surprised when I wanted more of her.

Lately, back at home, we were both pretty consumed with work, but with the season slowing everything down, and with winter nearly upon us, I knew we needed some sun and especially some distance from everyone and everything, as well as some time to be alone with each other.

She swam up to me, resting her chin on the edge of the

blue-tiled pool.

"Are you coming in?" she asked, looking up with those incredible brown eyes of hers.

Her nose and cheeks were covered with freckles—the sun had brought them out, yet another feature that I loved about her and hadn't been privy to before now.

"Why don't you come here, first," I suggested.

I needed her on top of me, now. She pulled herself out of the pool, wearing that tiny pale pink bikini.

It wouldn't take much to get that off, just the tug of a string or two.

She stood by my chair, offering me her hand. I kissed it and guided her on top of me. She straddled me in that slow way she knows drives me crazy, nearly making me come right then and there.

She started to rub on me, teasing me. I couldn't wait any longer. I pulled my shorts down and tugged aside the tiny piece of fabric that stood between us. I went in her deep, making her moan. I grabbed her hips and let her ride me, up and down.

I ripped her top down, taking her nipple in my mouth, savouring it, biting down just a little, the way I knew she loved. She slammed down, nearly making me scream.

Damn, she was good.

I held her ass—I loved everything about her, but her ass was definitely my favourite. She moaned my name and leaned her head back. After that, it didn't take long for us both to come.

She lay down next to me on the lounge chair and I held her in my arms. This vacation had gone by too fast, I told her. She agreed.

"I hope Max is doing OK," she said, bringing up her cat that was being watched by my sister.

"I'm sure he's fine." I found it so incredibly endearing how much she adored that cat. I kept trying to get on his good side, but it seemed he didn't like not being the only man in her life anymore. I liked the cat alright, but he seemed to go out of his way to destroy my things. "Now, about that swim?"

I knew she would say *No*. I could feel her body relaxing and knew she was moments away from falling asleep.

"Maybe in a bit," she answered.

I kissed her head and let her rest. Her hand was on my chest and I took it in mine. Her hands were so tiny, so feminine. As I stroked her fingers, I smiled thinking back on the previous evening and how she had looked. She was stunning, to say the least. Her skin tanned, her hair flowing over her shoulders, wavy, with streaks of gold running through—a goddess.

The sun hit the stone on her finger, making it glint and sparkle. I smiled when I thought back to how her face had lit up, the way she had started to cry and then had been embarrassed about doing so.

Of course, she would never believe me no matter how many times I would tell her, but the moment she said Yes, she had truly been the most beautiful thing I had ever seen.

She would always be the most beautiful thing I had ever seen.

And to think, had it not been for a picture my buddy had taken, all of this might never have happened.

ABOUT THE AUTHOR

MIMI FLOOD was raised in and around Montreal. She graduated in 2008 from Concordia University, earning a Bachelor of Fine arts, with a major in Film and a minor in Creative Writing. Mimi has been writing since the age of twelve but has only recently decided to turn her hobby into a full-time career. When she is not immersed in her stories, she spends her days with her two daughters and her husband.
They live in Montreal.

Made in the USA
Columbia, SC
17 October 2018